One Too Many Drinks
The Dignity Reaper

A continued journey into a world of
misappropriated Love and
unremorseful Sex.

George P Howell

Table of Contents

It's been six years since Geremy's escape, with no clues as to where he escaped to or who assisted him. Nevertheless, his Dommes wasted little time overhauling his brain to be Austin's replacement and join the ranks alongside the others.

As the newest of many serial assailants plaguing the nation in recent years, the public's faith in the FBI to apprehend these monsters was weaning. The thought that this world-renowned agency was clueless left Americans scared and feeling unsafe to conduct even the simplest of their day-to-day duties. How do you explain why they can not build a case profile, capture, or even produce a possible suspect for these horrid crimes committed across this Nation? Then there is the added twist, the Agency's failure to explain how some of the dead bodies of these serial killers' were turning up in public places, attached to them a note with their media given names pinned to them.

The public needed hope, the victims' families wanted closure, the thought of an unknown vigilante hero proudly tagged by the media "The Serial Terminator" brought forth that hope. A vigilante killer of killers, a cop's worst nightmare. Is this new assailant a friend or foe? Are the killings to protect the public, or is this another creep who just likes to kill? After this entity has disposed of the others, will it prey on the people next? Just like the old saying, " Be careful what you wish for?"

Geremy's reconditioning was complete, yet he was different from the other serial proteges; observing him, one could claim that his brainwashing was a complete success. His loyalty to his Dommes was flawless. Never had she had a subject who, when fully conscious of his new life purpose, excelled and moved into the role of a serial killer as proficient as Geremy. He performed his training with hunger and acceptance, obeying and exceeding every task.

During the first two years of his liberation, Geremy had minimal contact with the outside world. The first year, he spent very little time unchained. His turning was filled with being whipped, water-boarded, drugged and psychologically brainwashed. There was truly little time for him to think about anything, even Peter, except in his sleep. There, Geremy held firmly to the premise that the two of them would be together and dreamt of the jubilation in telling his son that he was his birth father. This hope allowed him to hold on to a small piece of himself throughout the sessions. By the midpoint of year three, he was honing his new craft.

The Dommes thought, for that, he required a higher form of acknowledgment. Perhaps acknowledgment mixed with pleasure. After completing each training scenario, she had him remove his clothing and lay down on the bed. She commanded Geremy to get his penis erect while she watched. Her Dominatrix attire was equipped with zippered areas to reveal her breast, vagina, and anus. Once he was erect, she would expose those areas of herself, telling him where and when to touch, grab, poke and suck, not allowing him to use his hands to touch her. She then would assume the cowgirl sexual position on top to maintain her dominance and seduce him.

Inevitably with the frequency of their sexual pleasures and his male serial killer assertive training, he felt that he was becoming her seducer. This feeling of becoming her seducer led Geremy to believe that he could use the Dommes' excitement and sexual joy and weaponize it against her, much like the letter to Dr. Isnov at the hospital. He wanted to use the same skills she taught him to trap her, replacing the letter with her sexual needs and wants towards him. He believed that he had instilled in her mind a pleasure that she could not achieve from her many dungeon-like playrooms. By the end of the fourth year, their dungeon sessions had come to a halt, no more placing the mask on his head or whipping him into submission. Those days are in the past. Geremy gave her his mask and asked that she keep it in a safe place, having full knowledge that he never intended to return to that submissive role. In offering his mask to her, she now had something of his to gaze upon, something to create a sense of loss and desire, a memory sensitizer—the student trying to taunt the teacher.

Her Frankenstein monster took the bait and began to feel more of a companion than an enslaved person. She asked him to address her by the name Helga. Their sexual seduction of each other was now unmasked and naked. Helga appeared anguished over their inability to meet in a public place. She allowed Geremy to think that she drew more and more pleasure in their sexual encounters, the perfect monster, a killer with a passionate demeanor. She had produced several serial assailants throughout the country, all performing some act of serial deviant behavior, but none of them could engage her in such a sexual entwinement. Perhaps Geremy was not wholly inaccurate in his thoughts of Helga's compassion for him.

When Geremy was released into the world to perform what he was trained to do, Helga's obsession for him increased with his absence. She followed his progression, reading every news report of his attacks, and longed for seducing him afterward. Geremy remained safe from capture by returning to one of the hundreds of safe holds Helga had around the country. Geremy felt proud standing on his own, and her role of Master over him was diminishing; unbeknown to him, this was all part of her psychiatric hold on him. The perfect monster must have complete ownership over what they do, the feeling of autonomous control - no need or desire to require the Master's approval. Geremy knew that he controlled his destiny, but he also knew that he had to maintain a submissive behavior to stay safe. After all, she was the only person keeping him from prison.

It was a dangerous game for the two of them, each having the ability to place the other behind bars, moreover, a death sentence. He knew if Helga thought that the roles between them were beginning to change, or if she felt the introduction of Jealousy, Betrayal, or Fear in their relationship, it would upset the balance they had, sending them spiraling to their own demise. This thinking was yet another subconscious thought buried in his mind by Helga to control her monster.

Overall, Geremy was not Austin. He did not enjoy the taste for necrophilia. Sexually engaging a lifeless body was something he found foreign and offensive, with flashbacks to Angelica. So instead, he created an image more diabolical to Austin – a killer who wants the presence of life in his kill. As he looked into their eyes, watching as they renounced the thought of this being true love and accepted the realization of no hope of survival.

This look is Geremy's devil, this was the look in Angelica's eyes after he had sex with her, and she knew all lifesaving attempts by him were now over. Angelica opened her eyes during Geremy's sexual discretion, and he did not stop. He watched, through her eyes, the shock and disapproval of his actions as all hope of being saved diminished. He could hear her thoughts through her eyes; How could this man, Geremy, that I still hold an emotional torch, treat me this way? How can you betray the honor and love I have for you by killing me?

Geremy was angry that she secretly married Harry. At that moment, the stories of death-drawn sexual joy told to him by Austin, along with his unfulfillable passions for this woman, were ringing loudly in his head, driving him to crave even harder that which was no longer his to have.

He was a man outside of his own conscious. The perfect killing ability that Helga was seeking.

Geremy's serial killing spree had reached the heights worthy of a media name, "The Dignity Reaper." Upon completing his sexual intrusion, he cuts their carotid artery and then restores their dignity by redressing them neatly. Well, that was what the press knew. However, there was another detail not released to the public. Sometime between the killing and placing the clothing back on the body, he forced a tube up the vaginal path and poured acid down the tube, dissolving any live sperm cells or traceable DNA evidence. It also removed any chance of an accidental pregnancy. You see, Geremy still believed that he had a son, Peter, conceived when he was making love to Angelica as she lay dying before him. He would place the victim's clothing neatly back on, the same way he re-dressed Angelica on the floor of the train. It was as if it was a way of saying, I'm Sorry!

To think that a serial killer would have remorse after so many deaths is absurd, but for Geremy, after each assault, Peter would flood his mind.

Peter, my son, 'I have killed many. How can you forgive me,' this daunted Geremy after each assault. 'Son, if you weren't taken from me, would I still be at this place in life?'

He blames Harry, Margarite, Carl, Stacy, Peter Sr., and Macie for the demon he has become. It was their denial of the truth that placed me here. Now I have to stay in the shadows, playing a submissive role to the actual demon, a woman who trains serial killers. I am so far below the tight rope that all I see is darkness, not even a dim glow of light when I look up.

 In the first two years of his escape, he often wondered what these once called friends were doing to his son, how they were brainwashing him against his true father.

Several birthdays have passed for Peter, and now at the age of 7, he has become an intelligent, full of joy, handsome young man. The family decided it would be best not to tell him about Geremy to allow him to enjoy a normal childhood. As for his mother, Angelica, he was told that she died fulfilling the most important and loving journey of her life, bringing the seed of both Harry and her into the world. Peter's security, family life, and the people he has grown to love are his grandparents, Peter and Macie; his father, Harry; his Stepmother, Margarite; his Aunt and Uncle, Stacy and Carl. Harry remained in the house he and Angelica lived together and married Margarite after Peter turned four. The ordeal with Geremy left Harry and Margarite with a need for security and seclusion. The location of their house presented the comfort of living a casual, unassuming lifestyle.

Harry and Margarite's wedding was magical. Macie and Peter Sr. gave the bride away, something they were not given the opportunity to do for Angelica. Margarite continued her modeling career, which has brought her worldwide attributes from her fans, plus a few acting movie roles. The wedding was flooded with the Who' s-Who of the fashion industry and some Hollywood notables.

Macie and Stacy helped Margarite plan the wedding, but as a top model in the industry, the pressure of selecting the wedding dress reached new heights. Top stylists and designers from around the world were bombarding her with sketches and ideas—all competing for the coveted prize of introducing this new bride and her gown to the fashion world. Finally, Margarite, Macie, and Stacy agreed on a provocative wedding dress collaboration by a well-known fashion designer and a newcomer to the industry.

The dress was made in a mermaid fashion, tastefully yet boldly revealing Margarites' shape. It was classically named "The Tulip." The dress was sleeveless, covering her breast while exposing her well-defined cleavage. The lace ran from the dress's tulip-shaped top, around both shoulders, to a high neck collar. In the back, the lace continued down the center, 3 inches wide to her waist, where it connected to the train. When viewed from behind, the dress had the flair of a traditional A-shape wedding dress accented throughout, with a small tone-on-tone worded pattern. The words, "Forever Yours."

Harry was dressed in a tuxedo of blended browns, and little Peter wore the same. Their shirts matched the color of Margarites' dress. Their bow ties bore the same color with antique white stitching that spelled out "Forever Yours" overtop the bow tie fabric. Peter was so happy to be their little ring bearer.

The family had reached a new normal. Angelica and Harry's wedding picture, which once adorned the entry hall, was switched with a wedding picture of Harry, Margarite, and Peter. A smaller photograph of Harry and Angelica's wedding resides on the table next to Peter Sr. and Macie's wedding picture. They've made it through the tragedy to return to joy and laughter together at home. Harry eventually returned to the fire departments' elite first responder squad, and everything was starting new, at least for the family.

Dave, however, was not of the same mindset of life-moves-on like the family. Instead, he had a different agenda. Geremy is still out there, and Dave could feel it in his gut that one day he would reappear.

With the cases involving serial killers increasing year over year with no capture or convictions, the top brass decided to solicit the help of an agent from the European office with specialized skills in capturing deeply buried underground terrorists, Special Agent Bryan Sullivan".

Sullivan decided to visit the scene of the last attack to familiarize himself with the attacker. That brought him to a little-known city called Donaldsonville, approximately 41 miles south of Baton Rouge, Louisiana. Donaldsonville was nestled on the banks of the Mississippi River. The victim lived in a house on the banks of the river. A small place in need of repair, left to the victim by her mother four years ago after her passing. Clearly, he wasn't lured to this victim for her money. Sullivan was puzzled. Why pick a small city like this where a stranger could be readily noticed, and yet no one could speak on seeing any new faces. He walked through the crime scene with Agent Chanda Valentin, a local field agent assigned to the case. Agent Valentin had accumulated a local reputation of always catching her assailants, tracking them down, and freeing their hostages and kidnapped victims. However, this killing with the other failed FBI investigations was causing the locals to doubt her. She brought this point up to Agent Sullivan. She wanted to know more about the what, where, why, how's associated with the overall hunt.

Before he can offer a comment, his phone rings, he shares the conversation with Agent Valentin, "That was a field office in the Florida Keys. They just reported another victim. They have a plane waiting for me." Agent Sullivan liked Chanda's skill sets and asked, "So tell me now, do you really want to know more and get more involved? I'm putting together a nationwide task force."

"Where do I sign-up." she quickly responded.

"You just did. We have a plane to catch."

They got into the car and headed to a nearby private airstrip. While on the plane, Agent Valentin asks, "What makes the Florida office believe this is the same guy?"

"Same MO, slit throat, acid wash, and redressed. "

"What's to say that this isn't a copycat?

"The detail of the acid washing was never released to the press? How long has it been from the last crime scene to this one?"

"Two weeks. "

Sullivan, with a disgusted tone in his voice, states the obvious, "This makes the 11th victim in 6 states, and all we know is he conducts two attacks per state, none of the victims have anything in common, he attacks all races, all sizes, all ages, and only women."

Valentin was shocked, "Are you serious? I had hoped that someone would have had more info collectively, and I was just being left out of the briefings. We need to do something quickly. If what we know so far is true, there will be one more attack in this state before losing him again. "

Sullivan receives notification that the rest of his team is in Florida and set up a command base. He instructed them to stay there and start reviewing statements taken by the officers on the scene, check all camera video in the area, and complete the background on the victim.

Sullivan and Valentin arrived at the crime scene 3 hours after take-off.

A few reporters were still at the scene while the forensic team collected more evidence and prepared for their departure.

Valentin turns from Sullivan and starts to walk away. She looks ahead and turns back quickly towards him, "Sullivan, Wait!". He walks toward her, and she directs his attention over her right shoulder to that female reporter in the blue tank top with the flannel shirt wrapped around her waist. "She was at both of my crime scenes."

"Go ask her for a meeting. Maybe we can compare notes."

Valentin turns and walks towards the reporter, "Hello, I'm Agent Val…." The reporter takes off running. Valentin follows in pursuit, calling out, "Stop, FBI."

Valentin radios back to Sullivan, "She bolted, running down towards the canal. I think she may have a boat docked somewhere."

"I'm coming around with the car," Sullivan gets in his car to join the pursuit.

The reporter runs between homes to a waiting boat and escapes. Sullivan pulls up and gets out of the car.

"Why do you think she ran?"

"I don't know."

"You said she was at both of your crime scenes; do you know the newspaper she writes for."

"No, I rarely pay attention to the reporters, 'they're like crime scene vultures, you sought of see them and not see them,' I block them out like unnecessary noise at a crime scene."

"But you noticed her. What about her attracted your attention?"

"I don't know - maybe my brain logged her in as a newbie at these scenes, one of the vultures I've never seen before. I don't know."

"Well, we're going to get to know her. She just made a new place on our poster board as a person of interest. Let's get back to the scene and see if any of the other vultures know who she is."

Valentin gives off a "sigh" as they get into the car.

Valentin did not want to tell Sullivan that she was a lesbian. He looked 'old school' and maybe would not understand that she noticed the reporter because she found her attractive. Back at the crime scene, none of the other vultures knew who she was. While Sullivan and Valentin looked for any loose ends at the crime scene, he contacted the rest of the task force and instructed them Priority One – find out who this reporter is.

It wasn't hard for the team to find out information on the reporter, they searched all articles written about "The Dignity Reaper" by a woman, and only one name repeatedly appeared after each occurrence. Judy Miller, a 24-year-old freelance journalist for USA Today.

Sullivan looks at Valentin, "Let's go talk to USA Today."

When they arrived at the local Florida office, they were informed that each office runs its own freelance people. The Florida keys freelance dispatcher looked up her name on the Michigan system, "OK, I see here that she was assigned the Dignity Reaper case nationwide by the Michigan manager. "

"You look puzzled by that. What's wrong."

"Normally, national authority is only granted to full-time staff journalists. You will need to contact the Michigan manager for any additional information".

The FBI office in Michigan contacted the USA Today freelance journalism office; the only information they would divulge was that she was a long-time writer for them and was presently assigned to the Dignity Reaper case. The manager stated that she had asked for this assignment. He gave it to her because she said she had the means to follow the story wherever it may take her, and we only payout when/if the story gets published. She gave us a phone number when she first started freelancing – that number is no longer valid. He also provided an outdated picture of her.

Back at the Florida operational base camp, Sullivan addresses the team, "All right, everyone, let's run through everything we know. Are there any commonalities in where the bodies were found, Bruce."?

"None, we have victims in their homes, on their boats, in the city, in the mountains.

"How about social media, Alice."

"The usual smattering Facebook, Twitter, various Dating sites but no links to each other"

"How about age and lifestyles, Carmen."

"The age range is from 20 to 45, homeless to rich. I've got nothing that may isolate a specific type."

"Take another look at their files. Let's take a deeper look at their home life, check for a spouse, girlfriend, boyfriend, pets..."

Carmen replies, " This recent victim had no one and no pets."

Valentin chimes in, "That's the same situation with the two in my area."

"Everyone, this is Agent Chanda Valentin, our new member. We need to check the other victims' files. Did the other women also live somewhat recluse? I'm assuming that answer will be, Yes. You see, Out of nothing, there is always something. The beginning of the victim's profile, living alone with no nearby attachments, no determinate lifestyle, age, or profession. How does our killer know they have no nearby attachments. He has to have the means to study his victims, looking for those that would not have a pop-in friend or relative, giving him time."

Bruce, "Time for what? "

"I don't think these were random acts of violence or one-night stands. I believe the killer needs to get to know them, befriend them and build respect for the person. The act of re-clothing them afterward is a sincere offering."

Bruce, feeling a little frustrated and tired, responded, "We already canvassed all the neighbors, no one reported seeing these women romantically engaged with a guy or a woman. The nearest relative was either dead or a day trip away, and no pets."

"We're asking the wrong questions. Go back, and ask the neighbors if they had daily contact with the victim."

Bruce, with a firm tone, responded, "Asked and Answered! - We already asked the question, when was the last time they saw the victim before the discovery of their body."

Sullivan gives Bruce a stern look indicating that he was not pleased with his tone and responds, "You're not getting it—still the wrong question. I do not want to trigger the memory response when the murders occurred or when the bodies were discovered. I want to know as neighbors how often they spied on one another. None of these victims were unattractive, and all were living alone. I am sure that someone was looking to see who they brought home or their makeup and dress style when they were going out. Find this in detail? We need to concentrate on whether she left the house dressed nicely every evening, only on weekend nights, and any noticeable changes in style? Understand the neighbors may not have physically seen the person of interest, but we may be able to identify a timeline as to when the victim met someone?"

Bruce's frustration slightly lifts from his face.

"...but for now, let's get back to concentrating on the victim's body. Go back in the files and look harder for a common thread in the number of days from the coroner's time of death and the time the body was found. Also, how was law enforcement alerted about the bodies? Collect what you can for a meeting tomorrow at 10:00 am."

"...and Oh! One more thing, figure out the time, duration, and distance between the killings. Hopefully, this will give us a grasp on if the assailant likes a certain time of the day and hopefully an idea of how the assailant may be traveling. That's right, team, Assailant, we have no evidence to distinguish whether this is a man or woman or someone acting alone. The media likes to give these creeps names. Let's not get sucked in and personify this assailant. Keep that in mind as we examine what we have."

"Morning, Everyone. I trust that none of you had a restful sleep last night. I didn't. I spent the evening thinking about the information collected from the field offices, along with the questions rifling in my head. As I am quite sure, each of you developed questions. If you don't have questions, then I picked the wrong person for this task force, and you should leave now." He waited a few seconds before continuing, "Good, no one left. Let's go through each victim's story from the beginning and work through all 11 in the same way. There must be more similarities."

Victim #1

CRIME SCENE INCIDENT REPORT	MI200704100	Location	Hiawatha National Forest

Name	Age	HT	WT	Hair	Eyes
Anna Anderson	35	5'5"	125	Brunette	Blue
Marital Status	**Nearest Relative**		**Distance**		
Single	Brother		200 miles		
Occupation	Photographer				

Personal Items at Scene	Wallet, Lip Balm

Comments
No known steady boyfriend. Body discovered by Park Ranger, Brad Dunn, and his Ranger dog @ 13:40 hrs approximately 100 yards west of trail number 327b	Grand Island Thumb Hiking Trail on a closed trail road W024B. Dunn reported that his dog was sniffing around and found the body. The Forensics team came on the scene @ 14:30 hrs. The body was covered over with moss, pine branches, and pine cones. As if the killer was trying to preserve it or protect it from predators and the elements. Pictures were taken. Weather conditions: 30-day drought with high temperatures, the ground was dry and hard. The immediate area showed no signs of any altercations between the victim and the assailant.

CRIME SCENE CORONER REPORT	MI200704100C	Location	Hiawatha National Forest

Name	Age	HT	WT	Hair	Eyes
Anna Anderson	35	5'5"	125	Brunette	Blue
Marital Status	**Nearest Relative**		**Distance**		
Single	Brother		200 miles		
Occupation	Photographer				

Initial Review of the body	fully clothed, the only sign of trauma is a round hole in the left side of the neck. No visual indication of blood on clothing and no apparent signs of struggle.
Item 1	Shoes
Comments	Women's. Size: 7.5, Color: brown, Type: Merrill hiking boots, Condition: not new, Appearance: scraped some soil samples for analysis.
Item 2	Socks

Comments	Women's, Size: N/A, Color: grey, Type: weatherproof and shock absorbent, Condition: dry, Appearance: no holes.
Item 3	Shorts
Comments	Woman's, Size: 5, Color: forest green, Type: REI - cargo shorts, Condition: pockets empty, Appearance: no rips or soiled areas.
Item 4	Shirt
Comments	Woman's, Size: small, Color: black, Type: jockey sleeveless tank top, Condition: good, Appearance: no holes, no soiled areas.
Item 5	Bra
Comments	Woman's, Size 32-C, Color: black, Type: sport, Condition: Clean, Appearance: no Rips, clasps intact, no soiled areas.
Item 6	Panties
Comments	Woman's, Size: small, Color: grey, Type: jockey, Condition: Clean, Appearance: No Rips, no soiled areas.
IR Overview	Nothing outstanding in the review. Clothing was sent out for DNA or any other foreign objects/residue analysis. The absence of stained blood areas on victims' clothing would indicate that the victim was naked at the time of trauma.
Visual examination of the naked body	
Feet	Photographed
Comments	Normal
Legs	Photographed
Comments	Normal
Hips, Waist, Vaginal Area	Photographed
Comments	Discoloration. Some signs of skin irritation or burning around the vaginal area.
Upper Body, Breast	Photographed
Comments	Normal
Hands, Nails	Photographed

Comments	Normal
Neck	Photographed
Comments	Exterior review of the neck wound, in agreement with the forensic report, no sign of blood on the victim's neck
Head, Hair	Photographed
Comments	Normal
Invasive Exploration	
Neck	Examination of the neck wound reveals pine settlements and wood fragments. The instrument used ripped through the carotid artery. Samples of the surrounding tissue extracted and sent for analysis.
Comments	This is considered the cause of death.
Vaginal Area	Exterior skin irritation appears to have been caused by some mild form of acid. The interior walls were also acid-washed clean. Tissue samples were sent for analysis.
Comments	no way to obtain with certainty that the victim was raped.
Lab Results	
DNA, Foreign Object and Residue Analysis	Clothing: The tank top revealed a second DNA structure not related to the victims. The second DNA was a match to Park Ranger Dunn. Ground Sample: The victim was killed at this location, matching blood found in soil.
Neck tissue analysis	The spectral analysis of the tissue revealed that the weapons' molecular structure was that of a pine branch.
Vaginal tissue analysis	Analysis of the tissue revealed a combination of household cleanser ingredients (Sodium-Hypo chloride, Sodium-Hydroxide, Muriatic Acid.)

Additional notes:

Ranger Dunn was called back in for questioning and admitted to urinating on top of what he thought to be a mound of sticks, exposing a portion of the victim's body. He changed his original statement that the dog had found the body. When asked why he lied, he could only express embarrassment in stating that he pissed on the body. He was ruled out as a suspect in her death.

Anna's brother was notified of her death and questioned. The news of his sister brought instant grief to his face as the tears flowed uncontrollably. He stated that he loathed the thought of Anna disappearing weeks at a time on photo adventures, mostly in remote areas, by herself. She's been doing this since graduating from college. So, to not hear from her for weeks had become the norm. He had no knowledge of her having a steady boyfriend or any man in her life. He stated that she was a loaner and could not provide any names of current friends. He was ruled out as a suspect in her death.

--------------------------------- End of Report --

Sullivan addresses his team, "for what we know. This subject is our ground zero. So, where are the holes in this report? Does it answer the questions we brought forward last night? Let me hear it – what are you thinking."

The team mutters out thoughts that are already clearly defined in the reports. Sullivan was starting to get discouraged in his team -when Agent Valentin spoke out, "Where is her cellphone? There is nothing in this report about recovering her cellphone. If she was known for spending weeks out there on her own, where was her base camp? Or even simpler, how did she get there? She must have had a car somewhere?"

Sullivan responded with excitement, "That's putting your mind into the scene, thinking in the victim's world. Here we have a woman who has survived living in remote areas alone for 10-12 years. Yet, no one in town recognized her picture, indicating that she stayed to herself. Did our assailant walk up on her, or did she walk up on the assailant in the park wilderness? I think she walked up upon our assailant. Let's call this assailant now Person-X. They struck up a good conversation, and she brought Person-X back to her base camp, one thing led to the next, and we had sex amongst the stars. I don't think that this was a one-night stand. I believe they camped a couple of nights together. The fact that there were no rips or stains in her clothing, nor any defensive evidence anywhere, states that she removed her clothing. Do any of you see this in the same manner that I see it?"

"Yes," replies Valentin, "however, to bring your story to reality, a few important facts are missing. First, if the body was found on a routinely patrolled area, what's patrolling frequency, and when was the last time this area was patrolled before finding the body. She probably intentionally picked that spot as a woman alone because it's patrolled. Secondly, the coroner's report did not mention any excess bruising at the entry point. So the end of the stick would have to have been shaved to a sharp point before the attack. That's premeditated and not spontaneous, which connects with your theory of shacking up for a couple of days, gaining her trust. Now, What I don't understand, if this was Person-X's first time and he used a stick and not a knife, how did the acid mixture and tube to administer it - get to the scene."

Bruce cries out, "Here's my idea on that! The body was well concealed so that no one would find it. Perhaps this washing was an afterthought, and Person-X did that so to allow time to take her car back to town and to pick up the items, mix them, and place it into her body."

Sullivan believed that Bruce's scenario had merit, especially if this was the first victim. However, due to the elapsed time of 5 years, it would be a wild goose chase to go back to the crime scene to prove it out. Besides, we have no description of the killer or the vehicle. So Bruce, after we complete the reviews, check DMV and visit the brother to get information on the car. "My guess is, Person-X used her car to get to his next location. Let's continue, grab another victim file and look for what's missing or assumed at the time".

It took hours to comb through the files.

Several commonalities were found in their review:

> No cell phones, recording devices, or cameras were recovered.
> None of the attacks occurred during or during inclement weather in the area.
> Video obtained through media coverage places Judy Miller at all the crime scenes, except for Michigan.
> Two killings were performed in each state after the first killing.
> After the first victim, a sharp cutting instrument or surgical blade was used on all the victims.

"All right, this is a start, Bruce and Alice. See what you can find from the first victim's brother. Carmine, gather information on how the police were notified of each victim. It could have come from our killer. Agent Valentin, you're assigned to Judy Miller – find her. "

As the team broke up to perform their task, Agent Valentin walked up to Agent Sullivan.

“Agent Sullivan, a word in private, please.”

“Walk with me to my car.”

“I came on board this team to capture The Dignity Reaper.”

Sullivan breaks in, “Who?”

She continues, “the Assailaint/ Person-X. This Judy Miller is not our assailant and plays a very minor role. Can we put someone else on her?”

“Tell me, something Agent, Why did she run? How is it this Judy Miller has managed to travel between states and arrive at every crime scene at the same time we do? Yet, we are unable to find any footage of her getting onto a plane, train, or bus. Nor were we able to get any face recognition at any gas station or toll cam between the locations. If she is not the killer, she travels in the same manner as Person-X, and by my assessment, you are the best person I have on this team to find that out unless you already have the answers on how she travels about. Do you, Agent?

 “I do not?”

“Well then, get to know her, and let’s catch this killer, be it male or female. Are you on-board?”

“Yes.”

Agent Valentin set off to find Judy. She started her search based on the information found by the other team members. She checked all hotels and motels in the crime areas. Not having a valid address or phone number for Judy, searching for credit card transactions was difficult. She searched all variations of the name Judy or Judith Miller. Five hundred possible names were obtained. A tighter filter was then applied to the five hundred, queuing on age, hair color, height, and body weight. The list dropped to thirty and was re-sorted by those married, single, and changed the last name by marriage or by a formal name change request. Out of the thirty, twenty were single, eight were married, and two underwent a name change. Valentin started with the twenty single-status individuals. We know she's here in the Florida Keys. The searched leads did not produce anything further to move on.

Valentin printed Judy's picture and went back to the house where she escaped in the waiting boat. After several attempts, this day, a woman answered the door. "Hello, how can I help you?"

"Hello, my name is Agent Valentin with the FBI. Four days ago, a body was found on US-1 not far from here. One of the reporters I wanted to speak with fled the scene running into your backyard, where she boarded a boat and sped away. Do you know, or have you seen the person in this picture?"

The woman in the house responded, "No, I do not. We've been away for two weeks. So, based on what you are saying – do you believe this person has been staying in my house. Do you think she may have been a former tenant? Are we safe staying here?"

"I am not stating that this person had access to your home. She did, however, have access to your dock. If you like, I can look around your house for any signs of a break-in. I seriously doubt that this person was inside your home.

"I would appreciate you looking around. Thank you. We've only moved in here a couple of days before leaving for two weeks and did not have a chance to change all of the locks."

"Is there anyone that has access to your home when you are away? Can I get a list of names for the people that have access to your home and the names of the people that knew you would be away? Did you announce that you would be away on any social media sites?"

"Certainly, it's only a couple of people, and yes, I posted a few pictures from where we were on Facebook and Instagram. Do you think she could have been the killer you are looking for? Is it safe for us to stay here?"

"At the moment, she is just someone of interest. I see no reason why you should be alarmed. You have cameras around your property. Are you backing up your data, or is it erased daily?"

"To be honest, we have not activated the service yet. We thought that placing the cameras around would act as a deterrent. You know, create the illusion. But, obviously, that did not work, if someone can dock a boat here and come and go as they please."

"Here is the email address to our field office. Please forward the contacts list there to my attention. Thank you."

Valentin continued walking to the end of the canal, knocking on every door, showing the picture to every household – no one knew or had seen her. The trail for Judy was becoming just as cold as our leads for Person-X.

In today's time of heightened security, one would have to be highly skilled or ex-military to be a ghost.

What is Judy's story? I do not believe that she is the killer, her presence started after the first kill, and she was in Michigan. Maybe she knew the first victim, and she's tracking this Person-X, or perhaps she is an accomplice, so our assailant is not working alone. Skills like these are not honed overnight. Let me change my search for ex-military special ops women with the same criteria. Valentin headed back to base operations to broaden her search protocol. As she entered base operations, Agent Sullivan cried out to her.

"Valentin, did you find Judy?"

He knew full well that finding Judy would be an arduous task, proving why he placed her on it. As they drew closer, Valentin reported, "All of my leads led to a dead end. I went to the house where she escaped in the boat – the owners were away for two weeks and just returning. The house showed no signs of forced entry. The owner will email me those names that had access to the home, along with those who knew that they would be away on a trip. Maybe I'll find something in that. I'm also going to check ex-military. Someone had to train her how to be a ghost."

"You bring up a good point, and with the recent influx of serial killers all moving about freely from state to state with no signature left behind, I think we are looking at a network of serial killers trained by the same person.

I saw a similar pattern in a few terrorist cells in Belgium, where a monitor travels independently along with the killing network. The monitor watches the actions and surroundings of the killers. If they appear to be on the verge of getting captured or jeopardizing the network's survival, the monitor terminates them. Go back and check the media footage of all the serial crime scenes from the past year to now -look for Judy or any person who appears at multiple crime scenes. Judy may be one of these Serial Terminators by design."

Valentin looks at him with disbelief and repeats his word, "by Design?"

"Yes, to maintain the integrity and anonymity of the network. Bring this up with the others and get them working on this with you.

"Where are you going? I'll be back in 3 days. You're in charge."

Sullivan was spot on with his assessment. Helga was part of a select few psychiatric physicians whose role was to help deeply seated covert government operatives cope with returning home. She was also on the review board for PTSD in American veterans, a group studying returning veterans' mental stability / coping mechanisms before releasing them as functioning members of society. They found that those veterans that had family members to watch over them or friends that stepped up as family had a greater chance for short-term recovery. Playing a role in this study was of great benefit to Helga. The other serial killers were all selected from this veteran base: ghosts, no family, no ties to anything, invisible in plain sight, and she repurposed them to do her bidding. Helga had created the perfect clean-up tool for when one of her Frankenstein's went rogue or was on the verge of getting caught. Geremy, the housekeepers, and the other serial killers are utterly unaware of the monitors and the deeds that they perform.

Sullivan visited a friend in Germany who studied psychic disorders and psychological, behavioral treatments. His friend told him of a scientist who perfected a technique similar to what was seen in the states. However, knowing this information still led to a dead-end. The scientist was murdered by a single bullet to the head eight years ago. His body was found in the smoldering remains of his home, which was deemed an act of arson, leaving no records of his work, no leads to any colleagues, and no information on any living family. The only evidence remaining was a paper and a crude self-made film of his trials and techniques. The use of starvation and adjustable pain level implementations changed the core aspects of the subject's behavior. The identity or whereabouts of this subject person is unknown.

When Sullivan returned to base operations, the team informed him that Judy was the only face found multiple times after carefully reviewing the videos.

Sullivan responded, "We must find Judy."

Bruce suggested providing her name and picture to the law agencies with a BOLO (be on the lookout). The team, with one exception, felt this would be a great idea, get more eyes to help us.

Valentin wanted no part of that, "If there is a squad of ghost killers out there, then by exposing Judy, it would be like signing her death sentence. She'd be of zero help to us then. Along with a new question - Once she's out of the way, who will replace her? Right now, she is our most important individual for learning about our killer, that is, once we catch her."

Sullivan agreed with Valentin; at the moment, Judy is our best chance for getting more information. "Everyone finds Judy! No public announcements, no local police involvement, check your contacts, but do not show any pictures of her or give her name out."

Bruce replies, "Oh, great, so what are we supposed to say. I'm looking for a ghost, and I think it's a woman."

Valentin chuckles and shakes her head, "Say that we are looking to speak to the people caught on video during our review of the US-1 crime scene. We're left with one woman we can't find. Last seen, she wore a blue tank top, pink flannel shirt, black jeans and black with white bottom shoes, approximately 5'-8", Auburn hair, and green eyes. Say nothing more. We must seem vague and clueless to keep her alive."

Bruce, "I still don't get it. If this killer of killers network truly exists, wouldn't they have seen you chase after her, as she mysteriously escaped on a boat?"

"I never caught up to her"

"Regardless, if I were the killer of killers and found out that you have included her in our investigation, then for me, she's been compromised, and it's time to remove her. Is anyone else thinking about this the way that I am?"

“It means we have even less time to find her.”

“Agreed,” said Sullivan, “so get out there and find her.”

Dave never relinquished his search for Geremy, but he also knew that he had to stay in the background to keep his family safe. He longed for his old life in the police force, and his wife felt his loneliness. They would sit and anguish over the impractical situations the screenwriters would put into television shows and movies scripts. His wife would often tell him to become a police consultant to the screenwriters. Dave was not interested. 'That's not real policing?'

After the Geremy episode, Dave's mind went to a dark place. The thought of this man, an accepted friend, raping and killing someone was beyond his suspicion. How could I have not seen the signs in all my years of policing wanted criminals? Dave became obsessed with catching Geremy and the people who helped him escape. He would sit in his home office and play out different scenarios, and the ones he felt were strong enough to follow up on, he would march down to the US Marshalls' situation office. This constant pestering won him the title of '# 1 pain in the Ass', even when some of his scenarios had enough merit to deserve action. Dave started bouncing from job to job, trying to find a good fit for himself. He so badly wanted a role closer to policing justice. The strain on their family was tearing at the very fabric the two of them nurtured since grade school.

Two years have passed, and Dave is no better. He started seeing a psychiatrist once a week, which kept him from worsening. Then a significant break occurred in his wife's protective status. The father to the son she killed in a drug raid was murdered in an internal power realignment. The new regime did not need to keep the hit request open on Dave's wife and had it rescinded. После смерти нет покаяния (There is no repentance after death).

This news brought great relief to Jasmine and Dave. They no longer had to watch over their shoulder. Dave saw this as a major victory to get back into law enforcement. Jasmine was not similarly inclined. She had grown quite accustomed to her daily routine, work, neighbors, and friends in Sacramento. The children are away in college, and with the fear of death lurking around each corner removed, this would be the time for her and Dave to rekindle their romance.

Dave applied for the US Marshalls and was inducted. He pleaded with the commander to be placed on the manhunt for Geremy and was teamed up with Marshall Rashel Ahrmen.

Rashel was brought onto the Geremy case after he escaped from the mental hospital. She was running down a theory she developed that his escape was orchestrated from within the system. With no supportive evidence, she was running up against one brick wall after another; like Dave, she was obsessed with catching him. However, her obsession was not centered on the person but the corruption within the current prison system.

Rashel was excited to have Dave as her partner. The opportunity to sit with Dave and pick his brain on the actual changes that Geremy went through with firsthand accountability opened new theories in her mind to be explored.

 "Hello David, I am very excited to work with you. The information that you can share with me is very enlightening. First, I would like to go back to the days when you and Carl were trying to perform an intervention with Geremy and his dark sexual encounters. Do you know where they performed his sexual transgressions or the name of his Dommes?"

"He never revealed that to us, and to be quite honest, we never asked. So, our focus was on redeeming him, and all blame was on Austin."

"Do you think that he may have told Carl?"

"Definitely not. Carl was so disgusted with hearing the acts of being whipped, pissed on, and forced to perform perverted sexual acts on men as well as women that he threw his hands into the air and cursed profusely. 'Why the fuck, Geremy?' He would say – wondering what happened to the man he knew, and then he would storm out of the house. I doubt that he would know anything more, but we can ask, prepare yourself to get a 'Hell No!' answer".

"When do you think we could go ask him?"

"Let me give him a call. It's been a while."

Dave called Carl at work and set up a time to meet during lunch the next day.

"Carl, thank you for meeting with us."

"Dave. How have you been?" Carl extends his hand to Rashel, noting to himself that this was not Jasmine, and greets her with puzzlement, "Hello."

"Please to meet you," she replies.

"Great! Come, sit." Carl was never the type to hold back what was on his mind and to have Dave appear before him with an attractive woman that he seemed to be very comfortable with gave Carl suspicion on whether Jasmine was still in the picture. Carl knew of the difficulty they were going through, sense Geremy but could never understand why Dave was so obsessed.

"Hey Dave, how's Jasmine and your kids? They must be, what, college-age by now."

So, of course, Carl was focused on the next words coming out of Dave's mouth.

"Everyone is quite well, and both kids are away at college."

"So now it's just you and Jasmine, back to empty nesters. That's great, Right?"

"Yes, it is."

"So, what are you doing now?"

"Rashel and I are partners in the US Marshall's office."

"Wait! …Wait! What! did you say - US Marshall's office?"

"Yes, before you met me, I was a State Trooper in Ohio. Jasmine and I worked in law enforcement and decided to leave when the kids started getting older. Rashel and I are assigned to finding Geremy and bringing him back into custody."

"Geremy! You want to talk about Geremy! after all these years. He left me with nightmares for a long time. What do you think I can help with beyond what you already know? Are you sure this is a case for you? look what it's done to you – loss of jobs, almost the destruction of your family, really Dave, are you sure?"

"I know he's no longer a part of your life, but Rashel wanted to ask you a few questions about the past.".

"Sometimes you should leave the dead - Dead."

Rashel asked, "You have evidence of him being dead?"

"He's dead in my head. But go ahead ask your questions. I'm not going to know any more than Dave?"

"Dave told me about the two of yours attempt to reach into his mind and bring him back to reality."

As Rashel talked, you could see Carl returning to that time. His body demeanor was tightening with each word she spoke. "During your intervention discussions with Geremy on his dark sexual encounters, did he ever confide in you by telling you the name of the places he would go or the name of the Dommes that turned him."

"Hell, no! look, sorry, guys, but I refuse to bring those disgusting thoughts back into my head. The stories he would tell us of the deeds she put him through still disturb me today. Sorry, but I can't shed any new light on what Dave has already shared with you." Carl looks at his watch, "I have a few meetings to prepare for this afternoon. Good to see you, Dave. Let's carve out some time to get together again and discuss better times. Wow! a US Marshall." He extends his hand to Rashel, "Nice meeting you, Rashel. Good luck on the case."

Rashel replies, "Goodbye, sir."

As they parted from each other, Rashel looked to Dave, "Carl seemed to be still holding a great discomfort for Geremy."

"There is always a bigger story to every story. So, that led us nowhere. Is there anything else on your list?"

"I thought we could go to the local sexual hang-outs and pass around Geremy's picture. Are you in, or will it be too much for you?"

"I'm all in."

"Good, there are a few places not far from here."

Thus, began a lengthy search thru what seemed to be endless sexual clubs, cafes, pop-up gatherings, and in-home parties. Rashel was finding new places all the time, but for Dave, this was an absolute dead end. No one knew Geremy or would admit to knowing him, in addition to the fact that he found the entire scene revolting. It was just as Geremy had described it during the intervention sessions. Rashel felt that they were heading in the right direction. Someone at these places has to be proud of turning him; we need to dig deeper. She enjoyed being the voyeur without having to participate, her own little Alice through the looking glass. Dave started to fear that she too would fall off the tight-rope and, like Geremy, be sucked inside this dark world. He expressed to her that they were going nowhere with this and should end it. Rashel took in his concerns and said to him that because of his close connection to Geremy and his previous attempt to break him from this type of behavior, it was clear that he would find this process offensive.

"Dave, perhaps you should let me handle this part of the investigation. My regular presence in these clubs is getting some attention, and patrons are starting to talk. I insist that you not come with me anymore."

"Rashel, I seriously think that you should take a break for a bit. I have seen the draw that these places have on a person firsthand, and I'm starting to see that in you."

"That's absurd. Our best chance of getting information is here, but you are right having both of us here is a waste of time, so you should follow another avenue and let's work in parallel. I'll see you in the office tomorrow. Go home, get some sleep."

"Are you sure about this? Look, don't go tonight. Instead, go home and put a plan together for me to follow, and let's meet up tomorrow. How about 8:00 AM, the diner on Arden Way, and discuss your plan. How about it."

Dave thought that if he could get her to relinquish at least one night, then perhaps she is not feeling the draw to come to these places, that this was just good dedicated police work. He did not want to lose another person to this world.

"You know, that actually sounds like a great idea. I'm sure that someone in there has noticed both of our presence, not going for a couple of days and then returning alone, may cause someone to ask me, why am I alone? Brilliant! And no, I am not meeting you at 8 AM for breakfast. I'll see you in the office at 9:00. Get some sleep, Dave."

Dave smiled, and she smiled back, realizing the concern he was having for her. She saw the pain in his face re-living the seduction of his friend to this lifestyle. She gave up the thought of convincing him that these are not bad people, and this lifestyle is their choice. No different from the LGBTQ community's sexual awareness or the Priest and Nuns of the Catholic faith swearing an oath of sexual abstinence. Meanwhile, some Priests are flogging sexual thoughts out of their minds, and others are abusing their young parishioners. In most non-Hate-based cultures, true believers wish no harm to outsiders. It's non-true believers who use these cultures to hide from their own fears that bring hate or misrepresentation. Like the saying 'one bad apple can spoil the bunch.' Rashel was sure that this had happened to Geremy and was determined to find that one bad apple.

Dave took this time to go home; Carl's voice asking about Jasmine and his kids rang in his head, triggering a long-lost feeling. He reflected on the days of trying to save Geremy and sharing the story of meeting Jasmine for the first time. How they stuck by each other's side through the good and bad times that's something that you don't walk away from without a fight. He entered the house, and Jasmine was surprised that he was home early. He looked at her with tears in his eyes, and she followed with tears of her own. Then, they embraced and spoke at the same time, "I'm sorry," in that instant, all of the woes left from their minds, and the stress melted away.

The special task team was still clueless, which led them to believe that Person-X must have moved on to a new location. However, the absence of a second victim gave evidence that he probably has not left the state, but what part of the state could he have gone. Sullivan split the team to have a faster response time. Each member went to different Florida areas based on their sketchy profile of the killer and victim. Before leaving, Valentin wanted to search some of the larger mangrove islands for Judy Miller. The team ruled this idea out because these islands were uninhabitable and would be exceptionally too remote for her to keep any eyes on Geremy. Valentin took it personally that Judy got away and was determined to find her in Florida. She hired a local fisherman to take her around the mangroves islands. The fisherman laughed and explained that you could be talking about over 200,000 islands. The mangroves are a series of vegetation-filled islands, some with passageways that take you deeper into the interior and others that you can pass straight through to the other side. He asked her what she was trying to find. Valentin responded that she was looking for someone who did not want to be discovered. Most of the mangroves are entirely uninhabitable. He suggested that they explore the bayside of the Florida Keys starting at Key West travel north. It was approaching noon, and they had traveled just off the coast of Islamorada Key when they noticed a boat that looked like it may have drifted into one of the mangroves islands. The fisherman explained that boats frequently break away from moorage during storms making this sighting a regular event; nevertheless, she decided to check it out.

The boat appeared to be empty, yet as they moved closer, the smell of death was getting stronger. What seemed to be a body was lying in the boat, and she asked the Captain to pull alongside. The stench was unbearable. She peeked in and saw a body in the early stage of decay from the saltwater and hot sunny days. The body appeared to be wearing the same clothing she last saw Judy wearing. She signaled for the captain to move further away and vomited alongside the boat from the smell.

She placed a call to Sullivan, "We found Judy."

"Great, you can take the lead in questioning her."

"She's dead. Her body was decomposing in the same boat I saw her leave in."

"How do you know it's her"

"She's still wearing the same clothes."

"How do you know it's her. I'll get our forensic team out there. Tell the locals that this is an FBI investigation, and no one is to touch the body. At the same time, run a new missing person's report for anyone fitting Judy's description. As Bruce said, the other monitor may have seen her running with you in pursuit, or did she kill someone matching her description to throw us off her scent. In any case, if this is Judy, I hope that her body will be more forthcoming with information than she was and if it is not her, turn this killing over to the locals after our forensic team is finished. I'm on my way back to you."

Agent Valentin called the local police with her location. She boarded the Police patrol boat and released the fishing boat that brought her to the scene. As the local enforcement approached the crime scene, she flexed her federal authority muscles and ordered everyone to stand down. The FBI forensic team was 10 minutes out. They urged Agent Valentin to allow them to pull the boat to the police compound area, where her team could do a better job looking for clues. It was a hot day in the Keys, and unfortunately, they happened to be on the sunny side of the mangroves – no shade. Everyone was getting pretty edgy, not wanting to spend time in the heat. Agent

Valentin had no way of communicating with the incoming team, so she forced everyone to stay in place.

One of the officers asked her if this body had any connection to the serial killer. Valentin replied with the standard answer; I am not at liberty to comment until forensics has made a determination. The officer took offense to that response, being fellow law enforcement officials, and walked to the other side of the cruiser. At that moment, they could see another boat approaching in the distance, just minutes away.

Sullivan was onboard and, upon arriving, asked that all the local officers move back away from the scene and take a position closing off the perimeter from other boaters. Forensic divers entered the water and checked above and below before constructing an inflatable walkway around the crime scene. The forensic team then went to work taking pictures and collecting samples. They noted that the boat line looked frayed, indicating that it broke loose and drifted to this spot. They stayed on the scene for about 45 minutes before towing the boat and its contents back to a remote staging area onshore, where they removed the body's remains and began the arduous task of identification. As they turned the body over, the victim's face was destroyed, apparently several blows from a blunt object. At first glance, this was thought to be the cause of death until a single bullet wound was found exiting the skull from the back. It was later proven to be the cause of death, killing the victim instantly. The blows to the face were inflicted postmortem.

Sullivan was confident at this point that this body was not Judy's. Why would someone who was sent to kill her take the risk of beating her face-in after she was dead, rather than sinking the body into the water and letting the marine life take care of it? The body showed no signs of a struggle. This poor woman was forced to change into Judy's clothes before getting on the boat, then brought somewhere shot and beaten, or our Judy enjoys the art of dressing dead people like our killer.

"Find out who this woman is, see if her identification was used after the coroner's predicted time of death. We need to catch a break in this case. Maybe this is it. No killer can be this perfect".

Valentin asked Sullivan, "how are you be so sure that this is not Judy's body." He explained that this was too sloppy. In his experience, ghost killers are usually former black-ops commandos highly skilled in killing, weaponry, and efficient in operating all means of transportation services, even SCUBA, Hang Gliding, Parachuting, piloting … you name it. So, with all these skills at play, why would they shoot her then beat her face-in with a bat. This body was left for us to find, to derail us from looking for her. Judy knew you were on to her, and she played you to give herself time to escape.

I am sure that Judy has traveled out of this area, using this woman's ID. When we find out who this woman is, we'll know where Judy went. You need to get to your next location assignment and get busy chasing living, breathing people. Let the local police deal with identifying this woman and notify us when they get ID confirmation.

While Sullivan and his field agents sort out to find Judy, Geremy slipped out from the Florida Keys. His ability to go and come with ease greatened his sense of being indomitable; no one could capture him or control him again, not the FBI nor his Dommes. His cockiness was fueled by the media coverage that he looked upon as being his fan base. A measuring stick to success, and the longer he stayed on the front page of the newspapers or the top story at the beginning of the television newscast, the more he knew his fans approved of his talents. Of course, he had to continue performing new and exciting kills to stay on top. But, to claim a permanent place on the front cover, something bolder, something in plain sight of the world had to be performed. He gave thoughts to well-known places, famous people, special events, anything that could permeate his name into the minds of his media followers. When he applied these thoughts to his immediate location, it became apparent that the new and highly advertised Florida theme park, "Virtual Discovery" on Lake Apopka in central Florida, was the perfect place. If the Dignity Reaper could close down the opening day of Virtual Discovery Park, that would be his world stage coming out party. Geremy imagined the headlines would read, 'Dignity Reaper shuts down opening day of the first large scale Virtual Theme Park.'

With excitement, Geremy set off for Oakland, Florida.

The trip to Oakland from the Keys was not without its share of perils, road closures, and checkpoints. It took a day and a half of travel, but once settled at one of the Dommes' safe houses in the Oakland area, he started canvassing the Virtual Discovery-themed hotels. Geremy wanted this Virtual Discovery attack to be an epic accomplishment with a themed hotel as his backdrop for the world stage appearance, but he found a string of 6 themed hotels and two wilderness camping/lodging sites. The wilderness sites, Camp Virtual and Wilderness Adventure, stood out as the best target points. These locations were prime due to their remoteness and ease in avoiding the surveillance system. He settled on the Wilderness Adventure Lodge and Campgrounds. It was the most remote area and equipped to house families in tents, RVs, or private cabins, with lots of trails and lake access. The killing and staging of the body here would be less of a risk at this site, but the media coverage would not hit the heights of front-page news. Think about it, leaving a dead body in a tent was not as glamorous as a room in one of the new themed hotels. Besides, a death occurring in a tent could easily be covered up by the Virtual Discovery Park Franchise. They would report it as an incident where a woman was found dead in her tent from a snake bite, along with a deeply regretted letter and a disclaimer on how they rid the area of all snakes. No, if this were to hit the world stage, then the body would need to be found in a very public televised/monitored place somewhere in the main section of the park.

Now it was time to find the perfect victim.

Geremy imagined this as his Hollywood set and wanted someone special to cast for the lead role; the victim. He thought long on what characteristics would be needed in the victim to launch his world presence. He carefully stalked the wilderness site visitors for that person. Targeting families first, creating destruction of the family unit by killing the mother, or maybe the oldest daughter would send a strong message. However, upon further deliberation on that scenario, thinking like that of a movie director, he slowly and meticulously pictured the steps needed to pull this off; separation of the victim from the rest of the family preparation of the body for presentation. Lastly, wondering how his fan base would accept this victim and this type of kill. You see, Geremy loved his media name "Dignity Reaper" and did not wish to perform in a manner that the media would rename him. He decided to move away from the family tragedy scenario, having lost his mother and grieving process. He did not want to put his fans through that.

He resumed his search, stalking the visitors looking for a single woman, a loner. He was surprised at the number of single women sleeping alone in tents for the opening day.

That evening while Geremy was sitting in the Wilderness Adventure Lodge Bar, mindfully reviewing his potential victim list, he was approached by Johnathan, a handsome man in his early 40's. Johnathan asked if he could sit with him and share a drink. Geremy was a little apprehensive by the strangers' approach, but as he lifted his head to look at him, he realized that this man was trying to pick him up. Geremy motioned to him positively, and the man sat down. He told Geremy of how he did not arrive at the park alone, but sadly, the companion he traveled with elected to dump him for a younger man just two days after their arrival. Geremy asked him if he thought his companion would come back. Johnathan was very doubtful of it; he said he saw them together, and they looked quite comfortable. Johnathan bragged about the size and the many amenities of the RV he rented for this occasion. Johnathan then smiled and asked Geremy about his accommodations. Geremy stated that he was one of the tent visitors to the park. They shared a few more drinks and idle conversations. After a while, Johnathan invited Geremy to come and see his RV.

Geremy, by this time, was seriously contemplating casting Johnathan as his victim; he's alone, a large RV for privacy, perfect. Geremy did not want to appear eager, so to stay in character, he declined with uncertainty. Johnathan stayed persistent and upped the ante by inviting Geremy to stay overnight with him rather than going back to sleeping on the hard ground. Geremy still showed a little reluctance with concern that the other companion would return. He questioned Johnathan on how certain he was his companion would not return. Johnathan, embarrassed, told Geremy he could prove it and shared with him the text that Breon sent dissolving their relationship. Geremy agreed to visit the RV but delayed the decision to stay the night. Quickly, Johnathan picked up the tab for the drinks, and they made their way over to the RV.

Johnathan gazed down at Geremy as they entered the RV and said, "This may turn out to be the best part of my trip." Geremy replied, "Let's not jump too far ahead. I've not seen the inside yet."

Once inside, Johnathan provided a tour and made drinks. He asked Geremy what he thought about the RV. Geremy replied, "very nice," and Johnathan quickly responded, "and me." Geremy kissed him and responded, "You too." At that moment, Geremy decided to cast his starring role as a man. Johnathan wasted no time in completing his moves on Geremy. He grabbed him, kissing him and groping Geremy's ass, breaking away for a moment to take a breath and to make more drinks removing his shirt in the process. Geremy followed, pulling off his shirt and maneuvering Johnathan in front of him, back facing. He kissed him on the back of his neck and down to his waist while slowly bending him forward. Johnathan was moaning in delight and anticipation the entire time. He quickly turned and stood up, unbuckled Geremy's belt, zipped down his zipper, and squatted, dropping his underpants. He moved his hands along Geremy's thighs and massaged his nutsack as he stood back up. Johnathan complemented Geremy on the size of his cock. Geremy turned Johnathan around again, dropped his hands to undo Johnathan's belt, dropped his pants down to his ankles, and massaged his cock. He then bent him over and whispered in his ear, "Are you ready?".

In a soft voice, Johnathan replied with a "Yes." Geremy rammed his cock into Johnathan's ass with unexpected force. Johnathan gave out a slight growl, "No foreplay for you, I see," as he reached his hands back to Geremy's thighs, pulling him in deeper. Geremy continued with his fierce love-making until ejaculating, and with a blow to Johnathan's head, he rendered him unconscious. Johnathan fell to the floor. The plan was to move his body to a more suitable place for the body to be found. He searched through the closet and dressed Johnathan in sweatpants, a short-sleeve T-shirt, sneakers, Virtual Discovery baseball cap, and packed a duffle bag with the clothing he was wearing at the bar. Geremy tossed the duffle bag into the back of the complimentary golf cart assigned to every campsite and sat Johnathan in the passenger seat. He then drove off into the woods. He tied Geremy to a tree closest to the lake and pierced his carotid artery. Unlike the other victims, Geremy allowed Johnathan to bleed out on himself. He then performed the same cleansing in Johnathan's anal pathway. Johnathan was an angry kill. Geremy felt no dignity in it. There was no Angelica moment, and it showed in the body. Yes, this was the world stage debut, and he wanted it to be different. He also wanted to prove a point and make the FBI look foolish. However, choosing a male was a mistake. Geremy did not realize how strongly his emotions would play against him without the ability to relive that intimacy he shared with Angelica on the train. Whatever the case, after Johnathan's demise, which took approximately 8 minutes, Geremy did not clean up the body. He stripped the body naked and redressed him in the outfit worn at the lodge he had placed in the duffle bag, including underwear. He then put the body into a body bag, and from there, he floated the body bag alongside his kayak and paddled along the shore of the lake to the Virtual Discovery main attraction areas.

Opening Day!

Geremy knew that prior to the opening of Virtual Discovery, all of the rides and attractions were tested and reviewed each morning. He would need to put the body in place after the testing to ensure that it would be found by the park visitors and not the park staff. If the park staff found the body during the park opening preparations, the Virtual Discovery Park Franchise would keep it quiet from the media. After the pre-opening testing routine, Geremy discovered that each section/area would hold a breakfast meeting. The breakfast meeting provided the time needed to position the body in place.

Geremy had reviewed the park's map and found that it was organized in 6 theme-specific 100-acre Dome modules. Travel to and from the domes was accomplished by a linked monorail network, enclosed and open walking structures, and moving sidewalks. Each dome could also be accessed individually, directly from the outside. There are minimal outdoor rides, food, and entertainment areas. The Domes are theme separated by Kids World, Race Training, Fantasia, Experience Sports, Wildlife Adventure, and Health Ways.

Kids World has an age restriction of 5 to 12-year-olds.

Race Training contains all forms of racing for ages 13 to Adults; Automotive, Aerial, Boating, Motorcycle, Skiing, Cycling, Swimming, Walking/Running.

Fantasia is for all ages. Imagine traveling thru time and space to faraway lands; Mythical, Real, Anime, and unlock ancient mysteries, fight evil foes, save artifacts from tomb raiders, battle beings beyond your comprehension.

Experience Sports, play team and individual sports; Basketball, Baseball, Hockey, Golf, Tennis, Boxing, Wrestling, Bowling, and more. You maneuver your avatar through the fields, wearing pressure-sensitive suits with built-in pads that simulate every hit, push and fall, all visually portrayed on the big screen.

Wildlife Adventure takes you Hunting, Fishing, exploring the depths of the sea and the highest mountaintops, hiking trails full of surprises, mountain climbing, zip-lining thru the jungle, and much more.

Health Ways was designed for those interested in Yoga, fitness training, endurance training, and more.

Geremy chose the Fantasia Dome for his world stage.

The first group traveled through the Dome with no sightings. It was not until the fifth group of passengers journeyed through that one of the visitors yelled out, "Stop the ride. Oh My God, Stop the ride." It was Breon who noticed his old companion Johnathan's body before him. As the rest of the riders became aware that the image before them was an actual deceased body, major pandemonium broke out. Screaming and crying visitors wanting off the ride, parents covering their children's eyes so they would not be traumatized, others running from the exit doors into the general public yelling, "dead bodies everywhere." The Fantasia dome was emptied, and the park was shut down, waiting for the arrival of the police. Valentin was in the Orlando area when she received the call from Sullivan. "Get to the Grand Opening of Virtual Discovery Park, a body was found. It could be the work of Person-X."

"Roger that, en route"

Geremy fled Florida before he could observe the media frenzy of his Hollywood performance. He thought it best not to be anywhere in the area for fear that the FBI would shut down all major/minor accessways, along with extensive searches on all of the tributaries.

Not having a specific destination, he wondered in a northerly direction. Along the way, he would glimpse television news about his Florida event, but to his surprise and confusion, the newspaper front page did not read 'Dignity Reaper Shuts down Virtual Discovery Theme Park. Instead, it read, 'Dignity Reaper Copycat shuts down the Grand Opening of the new Virtual Discovery Park.' The pursuing article described how this was the work of a Copycat. The media could not grasp the idea that the Dignity Reaper, the Fred Astaire of serial killers, dancing his female victims into their final good night, would attack a gay male. It was Sullivan that purposely released the notion of a copycat scenario. He wanted to deflate the ego of Person-X. In an interview with the media, Sullivan expressed, "This was a heinous crime conducted by a copycat. The person we have been pursuing only assaults women and is very meticulous in the gentle care of their bodies afterward. Our copycat here killed without reinstating the victim's dignity, leaving a bloody corpse in an area where children would be traumatized."

Sullivan told his team we must leave the investigation of this killing to the local authorities for closure. It's the only way to give credit to the copycat statement. But to make no mistake, this was performed by Person-X, and Why did he choose a male? Why was he so angry? Were we that close to capturing him?

Geremy was angered and tormented by Sullivan's media announcement. How dare the FBI take my best performance away from me and dismiss it as local trash, calling me Person-X. He needed to control his anger not to repeat the same mistakes other serial killers had made by sending a message to the media or directly to the FBI task force, proclaiming this kill as his. Nor would he return to Florida and commit another kill more fitting of the Dignity Reaper. No, at that moment, a wiser mind prevailed and said, Let it go! Your fan base did not enjoy your involvement with a man or how you presented him to them. Take the Mulliken, your do-over, and let the FBI's supposed Copycat take all claims of the many negative comments. I'll move on, allowing the image of the Dignity

Reaper to remain untarnished. Geremy did not take the bait.

Sullivan was disappointed that Geremy did not try to set the record straight, "Damn-it, now we've lost him until he takes another victim. Who the hell is this guy? And who is helping him? Everyone, go back and run cross-agency comparisons on what we know about Person-X. Someone must have come across this guy before. He's mocking us. This killing and this location was deliberate. He wanted to send a message to us that we cannot stop him".

The cross-agency comparison search came across a US Marshall's case in Sacramento, CA. Although it was not a serial killer case and bore no real resemblance to the FBI profile., it did have merit and should be explored. The case file identified a woman critically injured riding a train at the time of an earthquake with a childhood friend who decided to rape her and let her die after trying to save her. The commonality is that after acting out the rape, he re-dressed her neatly before being found by rescuers. Along with an unknown accomplice, this same guy managed to escape a psychiatric prison.

A meeting with the Sacramento US Marshalls office was set up with Dave and Rashel to discuss and review the files. Sullivan expressed to Valentin his concern that this trip could be a wild goose chase, but they could not ignore exploring any similarities. They left immediately.

When they arrived at the US Marshalls office, Sullivan and Valentin were escorted to a room with files already on the table. They were informed that Dave and Rashel were following down a lead and would return shortly. In the interim, the files before them were those of the case, and they were free to start looking through them. In actuality, Dave and Rashel stepped out for a cup of coffee. Dave also had his druthers on whether their case for a serial killer had anything to do with Geremy. So, rather than spending countless hours rummaging through and explaining information, Dave felt it best to have the FBI read it for themselves. Dave did not want to lose his case to the FBI. The entire office understood and agreed with the stall tactic used. Dave and Rashel entered the room 30 minutes after the FBI agents arrived.

"Thank you for waiting for us, I'm Dave, and this is Rashel."

"No problem, I'm Agent Sullivan, and this is Agent Valentin. Was the lead that you were chasing related to this case".

"We have many cases running through this office. I hope you had ample enough time to read through the case files. Do you have any questions?"

"Well, we sent you a briefing on Person-X. Did you have a chance to read through it?"

"We did actually, and as you now know in reading through our files, Geremy was not a serial killer. It was a one-time assault against a childhood friend he admired and loved but was denied any love in his direction."

"We understand that the two of you were friends. You worked at the same company and went out drinking a lot together. Did he ever show any anger or hostility towards women?

"No."

Rashel started to add a comment, "well, not in the early days but after…." Dave spoke over Rashel, "No, He never represented himself in a manner that would suggest a hostile behavior."

"I'm sorry, Rashel, you were about to comment on 'after the early days?"

"I've never met Geremy, so any comments that I may bring forward are strictly based on my interpretation of the case files before you. Dave knew him and could better answer your question.”

“OK, so tell me Dave was Geremy, a heavy camper or outdoorsman?”

“Now, here’s where I see a disconnect. When I would bring up going hiking, camping, and just roughing it in the wilderness, Geremy would respond If it does not include a 5-star hotel with an excellent bed, crowded bar, and a restaurant with a year’s waiting list, I’m not interested. Geremy presented himself as a model, from head to toe. Manicured fingernails, tanning booth sessions - the works.”

“Let’s talk about the day of the assault and the killing of Angelica. Why did he place her clothing back on her?”

“I don’t know if the question was ever asked. At the time, I was not in law enforcement. Check the psychological reports. Perhaps you’ll find your answer there.”

“While you were chasing down your lead, we checked, and it doesn’t appear that the question is ever asked.”

“Then, I don’t know what to tell you. Did he love her? He said he did, so I guess it was out of respect. Look, we have real work to get to here. If you would like a copy of these files, ask at the front, and they will ship you a copy. Otherwise, if you do not have any more questions, we're done."

Agent Valentin stated, "It is our understanding that you recently returned to law enforcement and requested to have this case. What is it about this case that is fueling your desire to be the one to apprehend a former friend?"

"Look, I catch bad guys, and this is a bad guy. Not to seem like we do not want to help, but we have a plate full, and it's time to get back to it. Good luck on your case."

They shook hands, and the agents left the building. On the way to the airport, Valentin says to Sullivan, "I felt like Dave was holding something back." Sullivan replied, "Yeah, he was just trying to protect his case from being taken over by us. However, If we successfully tag Geremy to our case, then our case trumps his, and the hunt for Germy falls solely on us. Based on the information in the files and Dave's accounting, this may be a dead-end, but let's keep it open. What do you think?"

"Agreed. There is something that Dave is not telling us."

Person-X continued his northern crusade, which landed him in the quaint town of Swiftwater, PA, located in the Pocono's. The perfect place for him to clear his head of those thoughts of grandeur and return him to the Dignity Reaper. He wanted his next victim to be a woman in her 50's, attractive, not very outgoing but could be found occasionally at a local upscale bar and restaurant. He stalked the restaurants that had a decent bar and a high-priced menu. Women in these places would be a little more well-to-do and have their own homes, usually passed down through deaths in the family. In towns like this, the women are in the middle age cycle of their lives when the children are grown, and the parents are returning to having intimate relationships with no restrictions. Amongst these women, sometimes tragedy strikes life is suddenly interrupted by spousal death, leaving them widows. Unfortunately, the same age group of men are looking for a younger woman or worked so hard to make it this far that an exciting night out is sitting on the porch, remembering when.

Oh sure, these women could quickly become cougars, and some do, but Geremy was looking for the ones that wanted neither the young, immature fools nor the living dead. He wanted the prowlers, the ones visibly searching in upscale social settings. He stalked the Swiftwater area for a week and a half and settled on Fransesca. She was gorgeous with a smile that would sadden your heart to leave her side. She was a middle-aged version of Angelica, and all of the emotions he had for Angelica started beating again in his long-frozen heart.

He approached her one night as she was leaving the restaurant bar, pretending that he was just arriving. He was dressed to the nines and held the door for her. As she passed by him, he softly spoke a question to her "is this a good place for a good drink and a good meal." She had already noticed him and approved of his appearance. Her departure at that moment was a test of his mannerisms, she responded, not stopping her stride, "Oh, so you are not from around here, yes, this is a good place." As she continued through the doorway, Geremy stepped out with her and replied, "No, I am not from here. I'm doing a cover story on the Poconos. It seems that every 2 to 3 years, in an attempt to drive tourism in the Poconos, freelancers like myself are contracted to produce a story. I'm sorry that I arrived too late to have the opportunity to ask you to sit, have dinner, and tell me your Pocono stories". Fransesca explained that she had only stopped in for a nightcap and that if the offer for dinner were still on the table, she would be happy to accept.

They re-entered the restaurant, this time together, and was seated. They talked into the night, and she explained how she grew up in the area, pursued a life away after college, was able to retire from corporate America at the age of 48, and returned here living in the family home in East Stroudsburg. Geremy was curious why she would travel 15 miles to this place. She explained small-town ears. I would rather drive the distance than be the focus of tomorrow's gossip. Geremy expressed his surprise that such an attractive woman would be traveling alone.

Her husband died in an airplane accident ten years ago, returning home from business meetings in the Philippines. Geremy extended his condolences. She thanked him and acknowledged that her husband was older than her and lived a good life.

"Well, it's getting late, and you have a bit of a drive ahead of you. Before going, I'd like to ask you one more question." She smiled. "Would you like to be my guide through the Poconos, make sure that I capture all of its beauty and mysticism?" Her eyes opened larger as her smile widened. "I would love to. What time should we get started; I can meet you at your hotel?"

"I haven't selected a hotel yet, so let's meet back here, say 9:30. Dress for a day foraging through the woods, comfortably."

"9:30 it is. I will see you tomorrow".

Geremy returned to the safe house. The Dommes had each safe house equipped with all practical regional supplies. To pursue Fransesca, he used the camera and camping equipment and placed them into the SUV in the garage. The vehicles like the houses are all registered to shell companies overseas, untraceable to Helga.

Fransesca met Geremy at 9:30 AM at the Frogtown Chophouse restaurant. She stepped out of her car, wearing a comfortable pair of slacks that enhanced every bit of her figure accompanied by an equally impressive buttoned top, with enough of it unbuttoned to reveal her inviting cleavage. Geremy was star-struck at the uncanny likeness to Angelica. He told her that he was not interested in touristy places. The further away from people and tourists would be ideal, to capture on camera the natural wonder of the landscape in the way the animals see it. Fransesca, with excitement, informed Geremy that she knew exactly where to start. Geremy bowed his head and motioned for her to lead the way. They walked to Geremy's car, parked around the block, away from the view of the surveillance camera. Once in the car, Fransesca noticed the camping gear and asked, Why the camping gear?". Geremy stated that there are times when the lighting in an area may not be the best at that moment, so he brings his equipment to be prepared to stay for however long it will take for the proper lighting to show.

"I understand, so we need to make one stop on our way if you don't mind."

 Geremy stated that he had all the supplies needed. "I want to stop by my house to change my clothes." Fransesca lived on a 6-acre estate with no security. The house is a 10-bedroom Victorian mansion. She invited Geremy to come in and make himself at home as she walked upstairs to her bedroom. Fransesca enjoyed Geremy's company last night over dinner and was looking forward to a full day together. As she thought more about the camping equipment, she wanted to know how well he performed in a real bed before the possibility of getting caught up in a tent. She yelled down to him, "Geremy, can you come upstairs and help me?"

When he entered the bedroom, she was on the bed with her blouse unbuttoned, revealing her bra. She explained, "if we are going to do some camping, I wanted to change. These jeans were easy to slip into, but I will need assistance to get them off." Geremy asked her to stand. Grabbing her pants at the waist, he pulled them down around her buttocks, down her thick thighs, and sculptured calves to her feet. She placed her hands behind his head, pulling his face to her panties. Geremy moved his head, pressing his lips against her panties, and exhaled warm breaths of air to her vagina. Bringing his hands up to the waist of her panties, he pulled them down and began kissing and licking her. She reached down to him, bringing him to an upright position. They kissed. She undressed him and was pleasantly turned on to what she found hiding under those clothes. She stepped out of her panties and slacks that were now gathered at her feet. He rolled her blouse over her shoulders and dropped it down her arms. Unfastening the frontal clasps of her bra, he dropped it down her arms the same way. Completely naked before each other, all that Geremy could see was Angelica. He became so passionate and affectionate with that thought that time seemed to stand still. Geremy was the second man in Fransesca's life since the death of her husband. The man before Geremy showed no passion in his lovemaking. It was as if she was another notch on his belt. She gave up the notion that she could find love again, until now, to have a man that was holding her with affection and getting more robust with each thrust, looking into her eyes and kissing her, they enjoyed the sensation towards orgasmic pleasure. She had thought, never to have this feeling again. For Geremy, this was how he dreamt each moment with Angelica, his true love, would be. Not like it was on the train. Life was giving both of them a second chance. They reached their orgasms together and rested there in each other's arms, neither wanting to disengage their embrace. Eventually, the need to urinate overruled their desire. They showered and made their way to the SUV to start their pictorial journey. She took him to the Pennsylvania side of the Delaware Water Gap, an 8-minute drive from her house. They smiled at each other the entire distance, neither one wanting to speak on the experience for fear of destroying the moment. The only voice heard was hers giving directions. She remembered the area from her high school runaway days with friends. They parked the car a mile from the main entrance and hiked in completely undetected, ultimately making their way to the Appalachian Trail. They pitched camp in an area with thick natural canopy coverage. Fransesca was surprised again when Geremy pulled out a collapsible fishing rod and crossbow. Geremy responded to seeing her surprise, "Well, we do have to eat. I have the usual canned and dehydrated rations, but I thought I'd catch us some fresh fish".

She smiled and replied, "So, you're expecting to stay overnight."

"Isn't that why we set-up camp. Besides, due to our late start, it's the only way that I will be able to get shots of the rising sun to illustrate how it wakes up the natural beauty of the area".

With the fish caught and photos captured, they returned to camp, and Geremy prepared their meal. Fransesca complimented Geremy on his outdoorsman abilities, another aspect she did not imagine from their first meeting. She went on to tell him, "I would have thought the closest that you would have come to being an outdoorsman would have been to pull over on the side of a wooded road to change the tire on his car." He laughed and exclaimed, "that's what roadside assistance is for." The two spent the rest of the evening with laughter and lovemaking.

Although this was the perfect location for the Dignity Reaper to arise, Geremy relived a time he never had with a woman resembling the one he raped and allowed to die before him. A real-life Jekyll and Hyde moment, which would prevail through the night.

In the morning, the two of them rose earlier than the crack of dawn to be in the right location as the dawn skies brought new daylight to the area. They walked hand in hand full of the promise that a new day can bring. Geremy was starting to lose touch with reality and wanted to stay in the Angelica dream he created. This day was planned. They would spend it together, discovering more on the trail to about noon, then press onward to the actual Water Gap.

The Delaware Water Gap has its share of wildlife; bears, groundhogs, cottontail rabbits, weasels, skunks, red fox, coyotes, white-tailed deer, raccoons, muskrats, mink, beaver, bats, and flying squirrels, all moving about waiting to be captured on film.

As they headed back to their secluded campsite, Fransesca tripped on the rocks, falling and twisting her ankle. Geremy lifted her and carried her back to camp. He laid her down on the tent floor and removed her ripped pants to assess her injuries better. Her legs were scarred with some blood. Looking at her body on the floor of the tent brought back the images of Angelica on the train floor. Geremy's dreamscape ended, and he knew what he had to do.

He wrapped Fransesca's ankle and cuddled up to her. As he comforted her, he said, "Easy now, it would appear that you hurt yourself, and sex now would only bring you more pain."

She smiled, hugged him tightly, whispered in his ear, "It doesn't hurt that bad," as she nibbles on his ear lobe. He carefully removed the remainder of her clothes and laid them neatly in the corner of the tent. He then removed his clothes and had sex with her, as he did on the train to Angelica. In the end, he sat up and pulled her close with her back against his chest, hugging her with the intensity that one would for the last time. He then kissed her on her neck, and as she extended her neck, he picked up the scalpel that he placed at the edge of the mat and severed her carotid artery. He continued to hold her as she bled out, and her body slumped forward.

As the Dignity Reaper, Person-X felt remorse for the first time for what he had done. He cried and slowly wiped her body clean, cleansing her vaginal canal as he had done with the others. While he redressed her, the visions of Angelica lying on the train floor looking at him continued flashing in his mind forcing him to breathe rapidly he needed to collect himself. He had to convince himself that the woman before him was not Angelica, his Angel. It took a moment for the vision of the body to change from Angelica back to Fransesca. He completed placing her clothes on and positioned her body resting on a rock looking over the Delaware Water Gap, a view that Fransesca expressed to him as spectacular. He then broke down the campsite and set everything in a blaze, and off he went using the same trails that they arrived in, never looking back.

The park rangers noticed the smoke and notified the park fire crews. The crew needed to put out a few other bursts that sprung up around the primary fire. As they contained and suppressed the direct fire through the smoke, nothing remained of the campsite but ashes. They opened a search radius to find survivors and found Fransesca's body looking out over the scenic landscape. The local police were called in, and pictures were taken. The FBI had put out a nationwide notice earlier that same day to all law enforcement agencies directing them not to disturb the site of any murders of this type but instead to call the nearest FBI office. Most importantly, do not move or touch the victim's body.

The Pocono Police notified Sullivan via text, "we believe this is the work of your guy," along with a photo.

The FBI forensic team was dispatched, and Sullivan notified his team to get to the Delaware Water Gap. Sullivan was in Manhattan and arrived by helicopter. He was the first at the scene.

"All right, guys, what do we have?"

"The fire was started over there, the area with the large scorched marks. We found some remains of what would appear to be a tent, nothing of worth for fingerprint checking, but it may be possible to pinpoint the tent manufacturer from a piece of the material and a local store that sells them. We haven't touched the body waiting for you to arrive."

"OK, let's go take a look."

Person-X took their time on this one, the best work to date. The victim looked as though she was enjoying the view. He even reapplied her makeup. Sullivan drew from this portrayal that Person-X either knew this person or she resembled someone of great importance to him. This attack showed remorse.

The rest of the task force trickled in and were all together by nightfall. Sullivan shared the pictures with them and made plans to visit the crime scene in the morning. He asked Valentin how Judy's search was coming only to get an answer similar to the teams' attempts to find Person-X, lots of dead leads.

Sullivan had a gut feeling that he wanted Valentin to pursue, so he reassigned the search for Judy to one of the others. He asked Valentin to travel back to Sacramento. "I want you to take the photos of this woman and present them to Dave. Ask him if this Fransecsca bears any resemblance to the woman on the train. Then I want you to go back through the files, collect the train lady's husband's information, visit him and show him the pictures. We have to get a break in this case, and this may be our second chance for one. The amount of care he placed in memorializing this woman is too much to let it pass on as a new dimension in his tactics."

Valentin, reluctant to go back to Sacramento, replied, "We also did not think that he would choose a male victim, but he did. Are you sure about this?"

"I am. I'm equally sure that Dave will lie to you. See what you can find out?"

Valentin left for Sacramento, and Sullivan assigned the hunt for Judy over to Bruce and Carmen.

Valentin did not request a visit. On her arrival, she asked to see David. He was surprised that she would just walk in on him, and he asked for an explanation as to why she was back. Valentin pulled out the photos and asked him if the woman looked familiar to anyone in the Geremy case files. In particular, did it look like the lady on the train? Dave looked at the picture, and his face went slightly stoic, and he quickly returned a "No" response. She asked for him to look at the pictures again to make sure. Dave questioned, "Why?"

Valentin explained that there suspect struck again yesterday at the Delaware Water Gap, only this time, he appeared to pay special attention to how he cleaned and presented this victim.

"What kind of special attention?"

"It was as if he knew her, or maybe she brought someone to mind that was very dear to him."

Dave, "I thought we were clear when you left last time that my guy was a long shot. What connection do you think you have now that you did not have before."

"I don't have a definitive answer, but your case is the only one we found in which the victim was redressed. Would it be possible for me to sit and look through the files again?"

"Knock yourself out. I will not be able to sit with you." Dave turns to the clerk and asks that Agent Valentin be escorted to a room and provided with the documentation.

Dave was meeting Rashel across town, the scene of another federal escapee. He informed her of the visit from Valentin, and she asked him if he recognized the person in the picture. Dave had never met Angelica and only saw the one wedding picture. He still doubted that this could be Geremy performing these serial acts, so he dismissed the look-alike story and concentrated on the situation developing before them.

Valentin found a copy of the wedding picture in the files and concluded that there might be enough points of similarity to get a reasonable comparison. So, she made a copy of the photo and one of Geremy.

Valentin returned to the PA office, regrouped with the team, and ran the facial recognition software on the photo. It resulted in a 63% match, more than enough to increase suspicion on Geremy.

Sullivan was ecstatic, "Yes, finally a fucking break in this case. Get back into town and flash this picture, of Geremy, at every restaurant, fast food joint, supermarket, mom-and-pop grocery, and bar. He has to eat and drink somewhere. Person-X is now federal escapee, Geremy. Find him."

Bruce added, "Should we also go to the local authorities."

"No, those guys have had his picture on their Wanted Poster wall for years. If they are not keeping a watchful eye, it's their fault. I do not want them to jump to action now and spooking our guy. His MO is to commit another kill. Hopefully, we get him first. Where is the information on Fransesca? Let's figure out how they met."

Carmen was doing the background check on Fransesca. She was born in East Stroudsburg. Attended East Stroudsburg High School before leaving for college, USC Berkley, California. She married shortly after graduating to one of her professors, Mr. Quatermen Alexander. They started a Distribution company for Telecommunications products; it became the 3rd largest nationwide. Ten years ago, during a routine trip to the Philippines, his plane went down, killing all on board. There was no sign of foul play. The accident was charged to weather conditions. Fransesca continued the business for another 3.5 years, sold it, and moved back here into her parent's house. She had a brief encounter with Mr. Douglas Evans, a local restaurant owner, ended in two years. Since then, she's been alone. Her neighbors say that she's a bit recluse, not interested in hearing about the local stories or going to the local bars. No dogs, cats, or close living relatives has a sister who lives in Paris - some freelance designer. She sounds like the perfect woman for Geremy.

"Since, according to her neighbors, she did not like the local talent expand your radius, maybe she didn't meet him here?"

Geremy was in turmoil with emotions emerging that were erased from memory years ago. Helga programmed angelica as the demon that ruined his life, yet seeing this woman and being intimate with her was like traveling backward, only this time his Angel was with him, not Harry and not the others through high school and college. Memories of a life he used to dream of, and once again, he destroyed it. Seeing Fransesca on the ground brought all the Dommes' teachings back, the torture, the pain, the beatings, and the embarrassment. The Dignity Reaper had suppressed weak emotional feelings for strength, invincibility, and control. He needed to find a new victim quickly.

Sullivan returned to the crime scene with the task force. Preliminary data from the forensic team indicated an accelerant was used for the primary fire, so the fire was deliberately set. The team concluded that it was here in the tent that he perpetrated the killing and cleansing of Fransesca. They viewed the cameras in the park and could not find any image of Fransesca entering. Sullivan queried the Park Rangers on any history of hikers gaining access to the park by means other than the front entrance.

The rangers smiled as they pointed out the massive areas of the park's boundaries not fenced. Densely wooded trees and shrubs define the park perimeter. Entry to the park can occur anywhere. They decided the best way to find Geremy's entry point was to work backward. Start at the burnt campsite and move east along the trail toward the entrance looking for tracks leading off the path towards any roadway. They were accompanied by two Rangers with knowledge of the terrain. The Team followed the main park trail and came upon several branch points with enough foot traffic to imply that it was used as a path. The team splintered into smaller groups to follow each passage. Only one led out of the park to a dirt road that looked well used by the community, where a car could be parked, approximately one mile from the main entrance. The forensic team was called back out to collect tire impressions and any other evidence they could find. No conclusive evidence was found.

After a disappointing morning, the team again had a crime scene with no lead-bearing clues. Sullivan knew he needed to boost his teams' spirit, "I just want to tell all of you that as individuals, you are the best of the best, and as a team, I could not imagine a better grouping. Geremy, in my opinion, is not working alone, nor is the organization that he is working with new. I believe this to be a deeply rooted, well-funded domestic terrorist group with safe houses, transportation, equipment, and these serial killers are trained in the art of espionage. So, how do we stop them? We need to stop thinking like we are trying to catch one person. We are pretty confident that for each serial killer, there is a terminator. So, let's get them to kill each other".

Sullivan rescinded his prior directive and had Bruce release Geremy's picture to the local authorities. He is confident that Geremy is the guy. In his escape six years ago, he climbed out of a cut in the psychic hospital prison fence.

Traveled down the block into a waiting car and got whisked away. That sounds like recruitment, and the US Marshalls have no clues.

Sullivan planned to hold a press conference tomorrow to flash Geremy's picture to the entire nation and expose our Dignity Reaper as the escaped felon that raped and killed a defenseless woman on board a train in Sacramento, CA. Next, I will give out the facts of this last victim, Fransesca, who was selected for her visual likeness to that Sacramento woman. Lastly, I will speak directly to Geremy, letting him know we know it's him and we are tightening the noose around you.

The people of Pennsylvania must be alerted. Send out a Special Announcement.

FBI – Special Announcement – Sullivan on the television

"Good Afternoon – We are proud to stand here today to provide you a portion of the profile for the man you know as the Dignity Reaper. He does not snatch his victims off the street. He selects them in Bars and Clubs, befriends them, dates them more than once before killing them. He prefers women that are: not living a very gregarious lifestyle, living alone, no pets, no close living relatives, few to no friends that stop by frequently. I ask that you take a hard look at the picture on the screen. We believe this to be the suspect. If you or someone you know has met anyone that looks like this picture, please do not try to apprehend or make him aware that you suspect him. Instead, call the number provided below. We have provided his photo to you because we want all eyes on the street looking for him. Let's bring this person to justice."

Sullivan hoped this blast would limit the freedom that Geremy has had and possibly raise the fear of his possible capture to those helping him and, Yes, triggering a kill order against the Dignity Reaper.

Sullivan was upset that he was an FBI agent enabling a domestic terrorist cell to execute a kill order on an individual. He thought to himself, what happened to this man to turn him so far off the main course, to become this relentless serial killer. Then Sullivan remembered his trip to Germany and that scientist studying psychic disorders and controlled psychological behavior possession. That self-made black & white film of a scientist affecting the core aspects of a subject's behavior through horrible medieval-style starvation and pain level techniques to produce irreversible brainwashing of that individual. The scientist convinced the subject that his beloved pet of many years was evil. Evil enough for him to drown it with his bare hands in a tub of water. Afterward, the subject showed no regret or sorrow.

The Dommes' brainwashing of Geremy was similar to the German scientist, using medieval techniques to place Angelica as a demon in his mind. An undertaking proved to be an easy task based on his disappointment towards Angelica. However, removing the boy from his mind was impossible. She could not battle against one of humanity's strongest beliefs – HOPE. The hope that one day this would end, and he would be joined with his son. During her tormented, psychological attacks on him, she never addressed his idea of having a son. She knew that this boy was his anchor to reality. When thoughts of the boy were flooding his mind, she could not get through to him. So, she needed a ruse to distract him, something he wanted near term. She increased Geremy's belief that he was becoming a Master, moreover, her Master, only to ignite the last stage of his change process. The thought that he could become her equal or control her became an obsession. Driving this obsession helped push thoughts of the boy deep into the recesses of his brain, knowing that one day she would need these thoughts again.

Keep in mind that with all wild creatures and Geremy was now a wild creature, you need a safe word, a picture, or an action to use as an emergency off switch when needed. Geremy's control switch was the boy, Peter.

Helga watched Sullivan's latest press release. Geremy's actions in Florida to declare himself an indestructible force against the FBI and his adornment of this woman in the Poconos was a flag to the Dommes that his conditioning may be faltering. That flagrant stunt could have exposed him and the entire operation. These were clear and dangerous signs that it was time to tug on his leash. Her dog has gotten too cocky.

Helga keeps real-time knowledge of the whereabouts of all of her demented changelings. Each of the serial killers, unknown to them, have an implanted tracking device. The safe houses are all well equipped with military-grade surveillance and tracking tools. They are all maintained and managed by a different type of Dommes-controlled changeling. The homeowners are psychologically defined as having a condition called Sehnsucht – the longing or yearning for something. For these homeowners, they long for permanence - a place to live that they can call their own. Some enjoyed mountainous seclusion, waterfront serenity, the city's clamor, suburban isolation, or back to old times-urban lifestyle. She would sort these subjects into three categories: The Silver Spooner's - born to wealth and spoiled by the decadence until a traumatic situation takes it all from them, in an instant. The Born Derelicts - children, born into generations of homelessness, and The Military Discarded - the returning home abandoned disabled veterans.

The housekeepers only know her as Helga and do not know she is a Dommes. They were never tortured in her dungeon. She was a kind woman with something they longed for and a promise. The control factor for the housekeepers is the fear of Helga's ability to take it all away. She explained that she traveled quite a bit and was looking for someone to live in the home and take care of it in the same manner. In return, she promised that they could live there for as long as they wanted.

It was interesting to observe the change in the behavior of each housekeeper when placed into a home. The Silver Spooner set back in a large home moved from a decadence lifestyle to recluse – they feared the term friend after their so-called friends abandoned them after losing everything. The Born Derelict, once the unseen, now has a roof over her head, yet wants to remain invisible to those previously considered as family and friends, for fear of them squatting at her home. The Military Discarded returning home with the pains of war still in their heads, no one to greet them, shunted and placed alone in a VA hospital, discovering that the battle image of the home they kept in their minds to get back to was replaced with solidarity, loneliness, and humiliation for serving their country. For them, this place became their foxhole, their trench, their field tent, their home to protect, their piece of the great American dream, only now they did not wish to share. That code and camaraderie that they once had - that no man left behind idealism was no longer a part of them, ripped from their hearts by the deep scars of public and non-public disrespect.

All of the housekeepers were mentally exhausted, easily manipulated, and exploited by Helga, and just as the serial killers had rules, the housekeepers had stringent rules to follow as well. They were not allowed to bring guests into the house but should expect to have Helga's guests arrive from time to time. Each guest had a particular passphrase. The housekeepers had no idea about the identity of the people they were housing and were told never to ask. Helga did not have any televisions installed in the house. Groceries and supplies were delivered to the safe-houses from the local stores and left in the delivery dropbox. The dropbox was accessible from inside the house. The same was true for the maildrop.

Each of the rooms in the house had a number associated with it. Helga would direct the letter delivery to her changelings by placing the room number on the sealed manilla envelope.

Helga sent a letter to Geremy, inside he found two envelopes. One read, 'Open this letter first.'

The letter read.

Hello Geremy,

I see from the news that you are now in Pennsylvania; I am so proud of you. I still savor the memory of getting together with you in Michigan after your first kill, driving her car, camping under the stars. Your ability to find perfectly secluded spots along the way. The thoughts of our naked bodies in the wilderness fucking like two Grand Elks excites me. You have gotten so much better in your lovemaking, confident, so hard, and demanding. I would like to think that I played a role in that, but this ability you always had; just needed to be freed. You are the Best of the Best, and I find it hard to remove you from my thoughts. I keep your face mask with me always.

But there is another reason for sending you this message. I have another well-earned reward for you. As you know, I have friends everywhere, and they gave me new information. So, please, open the next envelope.

The next envelope contained another letter and a document. The document was an official copy of the State of California City of Sacramento Paternity Report. He read the report and found it read differently from the one issued during the paternity hearing. This report read that Geremy was the father with 93% certainty. Geremy wanted to feel joy upon reading the words but thought to himself, why am I getting this now - this could be a forgery. What reason could the Dommes have to bring him this news? What new, fuck-with-Geremy, head game was she invoking? His joyful moment was turning into anger as he opened the third envelope.

This letter read.

I know you must be just as confused as I was when this official copy was presented to me. It would appear that your feelings for this boy in Sacramento being your son are now wholly justified. I did question my friend, How? Why? And it would seem that the parents of Angelica also have influential friends. They did not want you as part of their family or let you have any rights to your son, so they paid for the report to say Harry was the father. The manner in which they orchestrated this deal, having a third party knowing the actual results, would also leave them unaware of the truth if questioned.

I felt compelled to show you this information. You have come a long way from my days of manipulating you, now you are your own man, and we stand as equals.

So, let me be the first to offer you, Congratulations! And Condolences. Yes, you are a father, and I can only imagine the level of jubilation running through you and your need to raise the roof and shout it from the bleachers, but let's be real here. You are still a wanted man for the murder of your son's mother and now, although not yet unmasked, a very talented and successful serial killer. These are not quite the most outstanding attributes for a DAD.

With that said, you are probably wondering where the boy is, so I had someone locate your son and snap this photo. I thought you might want to see the fruit of your loins. Here's the best part, the boy will be traveling to DC on a class trip in 2 months, unchaperoned. That's right, none of the family members will be traveling with him. So it could make for an excellent time for a reunion of sorts—just you and Peter.

Goodbye, my favorite one.

The letter ended.

Geremy's anger moved back to joy, and with this new news, he was ecstatic about the possibility of seeing his son and being able to walk up to him and openly call him my son. He imagined the life they could have together, but first, he would need to clear his name a bit. He thought a good lawyer could overturn the rape verdict by stating the sex was consensual, a dying woman's last request. His necessity to flee the hospital was exacerbated by his instinctual desire to save his son from the dangers and lies of Angelica and Harry's family and friends. As for the serial killing spree, the FBI is still clueless, and no objective evidence to tie me to that person. If I stop now, it will go to the unsolved cases and be lost and forgotten. If they try to implicate me to the serial killer, I will threaten to sue them, and this Agent Sullivan will need to go on Nationwide television and apologize to me.

First things first – I have to get to DC unnoticed. One of the keys to Geremy's success was his uncanny ability to avoid major cities and highways, evading surveillance cameras everywhere, for if his picture were captured, recognition software would flag a possible siting to the US Marshalls. These were the typical complications he faced in getting from place to place. Especially now, with that idiot FBI agent posting my picture on nationwide television as the Dignity Reaper, everyone has a face to go after.

I must get to the most guarded, most monitored, and the highest level of security location in America in 2 months with my picture on television. Geremy placed his hands to his face as he thought of ways to overcome this obstacle when a 'true' stroke of absolute madness took over. They never saw me. The FBI could never place a picture to my name because although I walked through the towns and drank at the local taverns, no one paid any attention to me, I am invisible when I am the Dignity Reaper. I need to continue killing on my way to DC when I am the Dignity Reaper. I cannot be seen.

Geremy did not know that the Dommes was equally delighted with her message to him. The letter was a lie. The document was also a lie contrived by the Dommes. This letter was the emergency cut-off switch designed to flood his mind with the realization of having Peter back in his life. She knew it would trigger him to rush into DC and alert alarms of his presence, which would trigger his monitors to take his life. You see, the Dommes could not give the monitors a direct order to kill without reason. That's how she protected herself from them. They were tired of receiving an order to kill without cause, just for the sake of pushing political bias. So, she had them believing that her kills were for the preservation of the family. The family that she created for each of them.

Now it was time for her Frankenstein to go away, but unlike Mary Shelly's story, the Dommes could not let Geremy head off into oblivion. He knew too much. Something special needed to be planned. Something that her current monitors could not achieve.

Chapter 11:
It's Time To Know

Sullivan's news conference also reached the attention of the US Marshalls, Dave and Rashel. Dave was furious. What factual evidence does he have to entangle Geremy in his serial killer? He informed Rashel, "We're going to have to put your let's find the Dommes theory on hold and go to Pennsylvania."

"Why? Do we need to go to Pennsylvania?"

"Agent Sullivan just went on National TV without informing us and linked our investigations in his manhunt. I want to leave quickly and squash this. Are you good to leave tonight? You should probably pack for a couple of days. Oh! And can you please call that FBI asshole for me and tell him we are coming". Rashel gave a yes and had the office travel assistant book the flights."

Shortly after Dave's outburst, he received a call from Carl, "Dave is this news about Geremy true."

"I don't believe it is, but I am heading out to PA this evening."

"Well, I should let you know, Peter's class is having a school trip to DC in 2 months. Unfortunately, we are not on the team of chaperones. Should we have concerns about sending Peter?"

Dave kept eyes on Peter, and when trips came about, Dave was always there, somehow, behind the scenes. After starting with the US Marshalls, he would include these trips as part of his investigation, justifying it as a potential opportunity for Geremy to make an appearance.

"I will call you after I find out more."

Sullivan's little stunt to attract people to Geremy caused a frenzy of reporters to converge at Harry and Margarite's home. All media groups researched the tragic events of the train accident and wanted statements from the family. The television news stations talked about the details of that day and the trial, conviction, and escape. Peter was shielded from the exact facts of that fatal day, only now, to have his entire world turned upside down by a teacher bringing the whole tragic event portrayed on the television for current event studies. The class turned and stared at him. Peter ran from the room and called Harry from the bathroom stall using his cell phone. He was sobbing, wanting to know the truth. Harry rushed over to the school and blasted the Teacher and the Principle for their non-sensitive treatment of the information.

On the drive home, Peter cried out to his Father, "You told me Mom died giving birth to me. Did she really die on that train, and this man raped her? Why didn't you tell me?"

"Son, You were an infant, and as you grew, we thought it best to wait until a time you could understand better. We never had any intentions to hurt you or to lie or to keep this from you forever?

"But, you did lie to me."

"We did what we thought best for you at the time, but not with malice, with love."

As they reached the house and Harry pulled into the driveway, past the herd of reporters, Peter bolted out of the car running into the house, almost knocking down Margarite. She started to run after him, and Harry told her to stop. He suggested that they give him time to process some of this. Harry looked out the window at the zoo of reporters before him and spoke loudly to Margarite, "these bastards have no concern for the lives of our family. All they want is to sell news and improve their ratings, regardless of the destruction they cause to the innocent.

It's not us that should be bombarded. Go find Geremy–Question his ass."

Geremy resumed the hunt for his second victim in Pennsylvania, invoking the source of his invisible ability, not changing the pattern. He also decided that he would need to practice blending in and being more evasive for the bigger cities. That means being able to look (dress, hairstyles), speak(knowledge of specific city slang), and walk like city dwellers. This blending-in is all part of the Dignity Reapers' ability to be invisible.

Dave and Rashel arrived in the Pocono's in the morning. Dave was still furious about having to share the case with the FBI. As they arrived at the FBI office, Dave walked up to Sullivan and suggested a private conversation. Sullivan led him to an empty office. Rashel and the team could see them through the glass wall, they were screaming at each other, but you could not hear their words. Dave was still at odds with the idea of how this could be Geremy.

Once, a friend, cast out because of his unthinkable misdoings with one woman, now to have to believe the reality of him being a serial killer, performing the same horrific act on many women. For Dave, this was incomprehensible, and his only recourse was to act out in rage. After about 5-7 minutes, they walked out of the office. Agent Valentin was tasked to bring the Marshalls up to date with the FBI investigation. Dave explained that he did not want a blow-by-blow accounting of events, just tell me what information you have to predict the killers' next direction. Agent Valentin explained that this was one of the difficulties of the case trying to coordinate a reliable pattern.

Dave was shocked at what he declared their incompetence, "That's impossible; with the number of kills this killer has performed, you're telling us there is no clear pattern of travel. Get me a topological map and a location listing of all the killings so far". Dave traced the suspects' path on the map from the first reported killing in Michigan to the Poconos. The map showed a pattern, at first glance, that would support the consideration of two people doing the murders, navigating killings north and south while moving steadily to the east. He never reversed his direction...."

Bruce interrupted Dave, "Yes, he did. How else could get from the Florida Keys to Central Florida."

Dave asked Bruce, "Do you know how he traveled to get to Central Florida from the Keys."

"No."

"Let's assume, for obvious reasons, that he used the water. What direction is central Florida from the Key's?"

"North."

"I'm sorry, I didn't hear you."

"North."

"That would indicate that he continued in a northern direction. You also mentioned two killings per state. So, then this guy is not finished in Pennsylvania. I would think that he would stay tucked in the Delaware Water Gap Natural Recreation Area, where he could hike the wilderness or kayak up the river undetected. When did the last kill take place?"

Carmen said, "According to the coroner's report, midday 2-days ago."

"By the time we get mobilized, he will have 3-days on us. One more note, if history serves me correctly, the last time Sullivan decided to go public against this guy, wasn't that the fuel your killer needed to change his profile – killing a man in a very public area, the opening of the Virtual Park."

Sullivan responds, "that was a Copycat killer."

"Copy-cat my ass! That was your guy pissing in your face. If he has the same reaction now, Philadelphia is 100 miles south, and Scranton is 47 miles NW. Let's split up, Rashel and I will go to Philly".

"After all, your talk and mockery of our investigation, why are you going to head in the reverse direction? Is there some significance in the Geremy case that would drive him and you to Philadelphia?"

"Quite honestly, Yes, Rashel is a product of the Philly area. She was born there, knows the region, and is an excellent backpacker. So if he traveled the river down to Philly, she is my guide."

"Take Valentin with you."

"No, thank you. You will need all your boots on the ground with you instead of chasing goose eggs with us."

Dave and Rashel walked out of the building for Philly, and Sullivan and the team searched the northern Delaware Water Gap and all areas towards Scranton.

In the car, Rashel says to Dave, "What's going on, Dave? You know I did all my backpacking in the Sierra Mountains in California. Carl called me before we left Sacramento and informed me that Peter is having a school trip to DC in less than two months from now. If this is Geremy, then maybe he knows about the school trip and is trying to make his way there.”

“He's got a 3-day head start and is probably traveling the river. It flows southwest. That should place his arrival-time in Philly about this time tomorrow.”

Rashel had come to the same conclusion while Dave was talking.

The door opens, and Peter comes out of his room to a waiting Harry and Margarite.

“Hi Buddy”

Peter walks closer, slowly, eyes still full of tears and hugs Margarite around her waist. She runs her hand through his hair.

“Are you hungry? Want something to eat? Or if you want to talk – we're here.”

He looks up at Margarite, “I am hungry?”

“I made your favorite, spaghetti and meatballs.”

He smiled and went to the cabinet to get his plate, “Dad, are you going to eat with us?”

"Yes."

He proceeds to get three plates out of the cabinet and sets the table.

The mood at the table was a tense silence while they ate, then Peter broke the silence. "I want to know what really happened to my Mom?" he turns and looks at Margarite with saddened and confused eyes, wanting not to hurt her feelings, "My real Mom."

Harry takes a deep breath looks at Peter, "Your mom was visiting a friend whose mother had recently died. They lived in the house next to your Grandma Macie. This friend liked your mother, but he was too shy to tell her, so they never dated. When his mother died, your mom stayed up by Grandma to help him get the house ready to be closed for a while. On their way home, there was an earthquake, and your mom was thrown from her seat on the train. The lights were all out, and her friend noticed that she was not next to him, using his phone light to find her. She was barely breathing, and he began giving her CPR, and it just wasn't enough to save her."

"and then what, how was I born if you said mom died on the train?"

"I was the rescuer that reached your mom, Only GOD knows how, but she was still fighting to stay alive. Her pulse was barely felt, and she was unconscious. We carried her to the ambulance. On the way to the hospital, she started getting worse, and the ambulance machines were failing to save her. I had them take your mom to Dr. Sharindha, and she was able to keep your mother alive a little longer while they tried to save her reproductive eggs...."

"why were you trying to do that, re-po-duc-tive eggs??"

"This is a lot for you to try and understand at your age. Reproductive eggs are how mommies keep babies before they are born. Your mother and I were not ready to have children, so, for people who want to have children later in their lives, they can freeze these eggs to use later."

"you mean you didn't want me?"

"No, in fact, the complete opposite. Your mother had to go through a long procedure of needles and examinations to ensure we could have you when we thought we would be ready. Hearing myself say this now, it sounds ridiculous. It was because we did want you that we did this."

"so, how did I get here?"

"Well, when Dr. Sharindha examined your mom, she found out that you were not just an egg anymore, you were alive and growing in your mom's womb and that to save you, we needed to get a surrogate mother right away...." Harry reaches over and grabs Margarites' hand, "...and that's when your mom, Margarite, came to your rescue. She volunteered to be your Mom's surrogate."

"Sa-roo-got. What is that?"

"It's when a woman who cannot give birth to a child places that child inside another woman's body to feed, keep warm, cuddle, and bring into this world. Mommy Margarite became your first responder. She is our family's hero. Your hero."

Peter's eyes laid focused on Mommy Margarite, as his brain was digesting what he heard, "you mean, I came … out of your body?"

With tearing eyes, Margarite responded, "Yes."

"you saved me and sang to me."

"Yes, that was me."

Peter rose from his seat, walked over to a now heartfelt, emotionally crying Mommy Margarite hugged her and said, "Thank you, you are my mommy. Thank you for saving me".

Harry, too rose from his seat, and the family bonded in a big hug full of tears of joy to be alive.

"So, why didn't you tell me?"

"When...When were we supposed to have told you? Do you think you would have understood this when you were younger?"

"I guess not, but I'm happy that I know now."

With smiles on everyone's faces, Harry prepared to rise from the table when Peter said, "What about the stories of this man raping my first mother on the train? Are they true?"

Harry sits back down, and his smile leaves his face.

"Yes, Peter, the person she was traveling with did a terrible thing."

"You said he was her friend. Friends don't hurt friends. So, why did he do it?"

Harry paused for a moment, trying to figure out how to explain this to a child, "There are people in this world that look just as normal as you, me and mommy, but deep inside of them, there is a little piece that they cannot control. Your mother's friend had that, and when he saw her on the grown, and everything he tried to do to help her was failing, that little piece inside of him took over. I can not explain why he did this bad thing, and we may never know why, but he was arrested and sent to prison for it.

You heard in your class that he escaped and is doing bad things again; the police will catch him. We have nothing to be worried about."

"I'm not worried, Dad. I just want them to catch him."

"They will... I've no doubts.

I feel like some ice cream. Who's with me?"

Sullivan and his team could not pick up on any leads in the direction Dave sent them. Sullivan felt duped. Dave sent us on a wild goose chase. Unfortunately, he could not prove it, there was not enough intel to disprove Dave's hunch, and they continued searching. Sullivan turned to Valentin, "in the morning, head down to Philly, see what our US Marshall friends are up to."

Dave and Rashel started checking the riverbanks 5 miles outside of the city, looking for any disturbances in the natural landscape, looking for any campers along the way and kayakers. They found a few houses scattered about, most of them abandoned shacks – no occupants or squatters, and the paths leading up to these houses showed no signs of any recent activity. They pushed on. To the City of Brotherly Love – Philadelphia, they asked around at the piers, and no one saw anyone come in off the river, nor were there any kayaks present on the racks. They had the right idea, looking for signs before entering the city, but, Geremy got off the river 10 miles back and hiked in 5 miles to another convenient, safe house. He had just entered the city, but not by boat, to start his selection process, placing Dave and Rashel in the right place at the right time. Rashel turned to Dave, "if you were Geremy, where would you look for a date."

"The Geremy that I knew liked crowded bars with High dollar drinks – he said the price of the drinks would distract the low-income girls, and the music had to be felt."

"I guess you're buying, cause by his standards, I'm a low-income girl."

"I'll do you one better. Let's pop into this bar first. It's crowded, loud music and low-cost drinks, judging by the signs, full of low-income girls. We can relax over a few drinks, then go to the expensive places, slow-drink the rest of the night and see what we can find."

As they entered, a group of people walked in simultaneously, and Dave stayed back, holding the door. Rashel grabbed a seat at the bar. Sitting in the back corner of the bar was Geremy. Rashel caught Geremy's eye as she walked in, and he thought she was alone. He wanted to get over to her before she could meet up with someone else. As he started to approach, he heard her drink order - 4 shots and 2 beers.

Geremy paused, thinking she must not be alone, and at that moment, he saw a familiar face, it was Dave, walking into the bar. Rashel called out to Dave, "Over here, Dave." Geremy backed away to his corner. Geremy was happy to see an old friend, puzzled as to why he would be here and with this woman, where were his wife and kids. Nonetheless, Dave was a part of his past, and he knew that he could not have Dave see him. He waited quietly for the right time to leave. Luckily 5 minutes after arriving, Dave went to the bathroom. Geremy rose from his seat and slid through the crowd with his back facing the bar. Geremy figured that was too close and ended it back to the safe house for the night. He could not get Dave out of his mind. What was he doing here, maybe a convention or a business meeting? The timing of Dave's presence was too coincidental. Geremy became confused. I just learned about my son and now a friend from that past. He did not know what was happening, but it was enough to scare him. Geremy packed up his gear and left Pennsylvania without a second killing.

Dave and Rashel continued their plan and went to a rooftop bar at a prominent Philadelphia hotel. They stayed well into the night with no signs of Geremy. The following day, they did not wake until 10 AM and met downstairs for brunch, both sighing from the night before when they heard a familiar voice.

"You guys look like shit. What happened last night."

It was Valentin. Dave looked at her as he poured another cup of coffee, "I assume Sullivan sent you."

"Yeah, Sullivan figured out that you probably duped him. So, what's the plan?"

"The plan! Why are you here?"

"Come on; it's just the three of us now. Let's work together. I don't care who gets the credit. I want this guy stopped."

"I have to go hit the john, Rashel, fill her in on our plans here in Philadelphia."

That was Dave's way of telling Rashel to inform Valentin only of our plans to bar hop and not tell her anything about the school trip to DC.

Rashel explained the plan; "Dave said that Geremy liked places with big crowds, loud music, expensive drinks, and women with their noses up their asses."

"What?"

"Well, he didn't say noses up their ass. Geremy did not like low-income girls."

"Oh! well, that's completely against the profiles that we put together on his victims."

"Another reason why Dave and I cannot put 2 and 2 together on why Sullivan is stuck on Geremy. Our guy does not match your profile."

"If that's true, then why are you here?"

"By Sullivan making that announcement to the press, he arbitrarily linked our two cases. We are here to discredit the announcement."

"So, what happens, say, the bar he goes to tonight is the one you went to last night and again tomorrow night?"

"We checked the surveillance cameras to ensure they were operational; we also informed the owner that we would be back to see each night's footage. The owner has our cards with instructions to call in if they see him."

" You told the owner that we are looking for the Dignity Reaper?"

"We're the US Marshalls. Our guy is a federal escapee, not the Dignity Reaper. Understand, the businesses here are accustomed to getting our type of escapee request, with a detention and correctional facility located 10 miles upriver."

Dave returns, "Alrighty, I'm sure Rashel has thoroughly brought you up to speed on what we are planning. So what are your plans here?"

"I thought I would tag along with you."

"No, we do not need a team of FBI agents storming the area."

"Not the team, just me. Another set of eyes can't hurt."

"An extra set of eyes, not a bad idea."

Valentin suggests, "What if we split up and each of us take on a different bar?"

"I can see that, but under strict rules, no one moves in on their own. If you see Geremy step outside, call the others and just survey until we join. Clear?"

"Clear!"

"Clear!"

"Let's go pick out the clubs of choice and prepare for tonight."

Valentin calls Sullivan to bring him up to speed on the plan. She also expressed Dave's lack of trust in the bureau. Sullivan disagrees based on the many profiles that they have put together. "All of our victim's profiles', except for Fransesca, would suggest that he would be looking for a low-income girl." Sullivan did like the idea of targeting the bars and had his team do the same, concentrating on the low-income girl spots. He told Valentin that he would leave immediately to travel down to Philly and pick up the search spots focusing on low-income girl hang-outs. He instructed Valentin to stay with the Marshalls and keep building their trust.

They visited the bars and reviewed the footage for the next two days with no leads or sightings. Sullivan convinced his team was on a goose chase, instructed them to meet at the local FBI office in Philadelphia. Sullivan addressed them, excluding the Marshallsthe next day, "I think we lost him. Something must have spoked him. Any thoughts?"

Carmen speaks, "Looking at all the data, he has always moved forward with a second killing, even to the point of just bringing insult to our investigation. If I have to think about what's changed, I contribute it to two factors; the first is the presence of the US Marshalls and the second would be increased insecurity, brought about by being in a city setting (many people, lots of cameras everywhere).”

“If we go with your first hunch. Do you think the Marshalls saw him and tipped him off?”

“No, I’m thinking the opposite. Dave and Geremy were friends, worked together, drank together, they knew each other very well. What if Geremy saw Dave? It would confuse me enough to want to get out of town; face the facts, we are a long way from Sacramento.”

“So, where do you think this view of Dave took place?”

“It would have to have been here in Philly. I’m certain that Geremy was gone from the Pocono crime scene by the time the Marshalls arrived, and they left the crime scene straight to here.”

Valentin was intrigued, “If that’s true, outside of the first night, we should only have to view the footage of the bars Dave went to.” Geremy doesn’t know Rashel.

“Yes, unless he stopped in at another bar, one that he was not looking for Geremy in. Valentin, get back with the Marshalls and test out Carmen’s theory, tell them these high-class bars are getting expensive and if they knew of a bar that they could get cheaper drinks and regroup.”

Valentin returned to her room and waited there past the morning meet-up time. Rashel called her phone, "Hey, are you OK."

"Yeah, last night was a little rougher than I thought."

"Are you coming to brunch?"

"On my way, have coffee ready."

Rashel relays the message to Dave that she is on her way. Valentin changed her clothes and muddled her hair.

"Good Morning"

Dave replied, "I thought you FEDs were tough. What happened last night?"

"This is what happens when you don't refuse any drinks bought for you at the bar."

They all laughed. Dave pours her a cup of coffee.

"Go ahead and laugh, but I did have a new idea this morning. We have been at this for two days. What if instead of us seeing Geremy, do you think he could have seen us, in particular, you Dave. Do you think he would still recognize you? And if he did, would it spook him enough to leave the area?"

" Yes, I believe if he saw me today that he would recognize me. With that said, the cameras would have caught him outside of the bar. I did not see him in any of the footage we reviewed."

"Unless he saw you at a different bar. Have you or the two of you stopped at any other bars since you arrived?"

"You're aware of all the upscale bars that we've been to." Rashel talks over Dave, "Except… that crowded bar we stopped in before going to the first upscale place."

"Yes, but that would not have been his regular hang-out."

Valentin, "Not back when you knew him. Maybe he's changed. He is a wanted felon. Where would he get the money to frequent the high-class types of places?"

Rashel, "Your right. We should go back to that bar and pull the videos for that night and every night leading to today."

Dave, "Eat up and go get dressed."

They woke up the bar owner and met him at the location. As they reviewed the tapes, the outside camera caught someone in a hoody that looked somewhat like Geremy entering before they arrived. The inside cameras caught Geremy moving toward Rashel, then turning quickly away as Dave approached. It was Geremy. The following evening videos did not reveal any more footage of Geremy, but it did show someone else of interest, Sullivan.

Dave, "How long has he been here? Maybe Geremy saw him?"

Valentin, "He arrived last night."

"and the rest of the team?"

"They arrived this morning."

"So, you weren't late because of a hard night. You met with your team this morning, didn't you?"

"Yes, but let's not get away from the facts. Geremy was here. Your plan for checking the bars was correct, only his style has changed, and by him being here, it is validation that he is our serial killer, and now we've lost him again. We need to work together."

"It looks like your right. Where is your team now?

"At the local office."

"OK, you go, and we'll go check out and meet you there?"

After Valentin left, Rashel asked Dave, "Are you going to tell them about Peter?"

"No way, my resolve is to keep Peter safe. These yahoos would want to place protective custody around Peter and use him as a decoy, then if / when things go a little sideways, the shooting begins. I am not going to let that happen. We keep that information to us, agreed?"

"Agreed."

"OK, let's see what plan they've brewed up for us."

"Are you going to try and steer them away again?"

"No, this time, we can use their help. If we can catch Geremy before DC, we all win."

As Dave and Rashel entered the room, Sullivan lashed out, screaming, "you obstructed a federal investigation. I should have you locked up. What do you have to say for yourself?"

"Nothing. We discussed a plausible idea and divided the territory between the teams to pursue it. What are you yelling about?"

"We had him, YOU! had him and let him get away."

"and how many times have you lost him? At least we know a little more about his hunting styles. However, once again, he is a couple of days ahead of us to his next location. I still believe that he will use the river for transportation, which would open up Delaware and Maryland."

Sullivan exclaims, "I'll send a chopper to search the rivers."

"That's not a good idea. A helicopter in that setting can be heard from miles away. You'll chase him off the river and into the woods. The terrain there is far too dense and too wide to track. Keeping him in the river should bring us better visibility and centralize his movement. Let's send part of this team to camp out at the river by the Delaware – Maryland border. This group will be our catch net if he stops in Delaware for a kill and tries to get out. I suggest the rest of you break down into one-person units and attack as many bars as possible."

Sullivan spoke in a decisive voice, "Sounds good, except you're not going to be there. If he sees you, he might run again."

"Let me first remind you that you do not command the US Marshalls Office. Our charge here is for the recapture of a prison escapee. You can continue your pursuit of a serial killer in parallel. Second, your face has been plastered across nationwide television. What if he sees you? Plus, Geremy doesn't know that I am a US Marshall, but now is not the time for us to be bantering. Let's work together and move out before placing more time and distance in our path. Rashel and I will camp out at the border."

The meeting ends, and the teams get into their vehicles and head for Delaware.

Rashel, "What was all that about? You wanted to camp out at the border."

Dave, "I know, but if I had just come out with that, Sullivan would have thought I was trying to dupe him again."

Rashel laughed. Off they went and camped out at the Maryland state-line, ready to catch Geremy if he evaded the Delaware team. The main concern was that Geremy was getting closer to DC, and Dave knew he had to stop him, and this seemed like the best place to do that. Valentin accompanied Dave and Rashel in the camp-out, touting something about not wanting to break up the team we started.

Delaware did not become the shining capture point that they were planning. Geremy, seeing Dave at the bar, decided to stop the killing. He remembered how hard Dave worked with him to rid him of the Dommes. Geremy also remembered the story Dave told, during the intervention, on how he met his wife, Jasmine, and how it touched his heart to hear of such a committed love between two people. Geremy felt that same love and emotional connection for this boy. He suffered over the thought of touching his son with hands bloodier than they are already. Seeing Dave gave him the strength of a new beginning, swearing off taking another life while paddling his kayak from the Delaware River into the Atlantic Ocean. The spectacle of the river mouth opening into the vastness of the ocean on a clear and crisp early morning sky was a view he thought would make even an Angel shed a tear. Geremy was finally at peace from the Dommes, and he knew meeting his son would be his destiny.

The team executed the Bar plan in Wilmington, Delaware, without results. The next day they were going to view as much camera footage as possible before resuming again. They called down to Valentin, reporting that there were zero sightings of Geremy on the first grouping videos. That evening Valentin received a hit on the Find Judy tip line she had created. She was cited in Easton Shores, MD. She shouted to Dave and Rashel, "we have to pack up."

Rashel looked at her and asked, "why?"

"He's in Easton Shores, MD."

"Who?"

"Geremy"

Dave immediately jumped up, "Why did you say that? How do you know?"

"I received a tip on a person that I marked as a person of interest. She was seen there, and wherever she is, so is Geremy. I'll explain in the car."

Dave did not want to waste any more time and had zero concern about the camping equipment. He told the team," get in the car, and let's get moving." He said to Valentin, "now, how do you know this?"

We've been working under this theory of Sullivan's, that these killers are organized and working like terrorist cells. Each cell has a serial killer and a monitor. The monitor's job is to terminate the serial killer before they get caught or give out any information on the cell. Sullivan also thinks that the monitor may also have a terminator."

Dave looked at Valentin as if she said little green men were walking the earth, "Are you serious? Why would he think that?"

"Over the last five years, haven't you noticed the increase in serial type killings."

"Yes, but you have also had success in stopping them."

Rashel, "No, they haven't, Dave, their bodies have been found with notes, markings, or a newspaper article identifying which serial killer they are."

Dave was surprised that Rashel was informed, "You know this, How?"

"I became interested three years ago, and I agree with Sullivan, this is domestic terrorism."

"Well, I guess I've been living under a rock consumed with my own terrors. Do you have any proof of this theory?"

"At the Florida crime scene, I noticed a reporter that I had seen at multiple crime scenes involving Geremy. Sullivan suggested that I should talk to her to compare notes. As I walked toward her, she bolted, running down a canal jumping onto a waiting boat. She escaped. I was tasked to find her, and I thought I was getting close and chased her out to some of the barrier islands. I charted a local fishing boat to search the outer islands along the Florida Keys. We came upon a boat that had broken off its moorings and drifted into the mangroves. Inside was a woman's body, the same size, weight, hair color, and wearing the same clothes as my person of interest when last seen. Examination of the body revealed that this woman had been shot and then clubbed in the face. That woman inside was killed and dressed up like Judy to derail my investigation. It was evident that Judy was definitely, not just a reporter."

"So, this tip was about your Judy."

"Yes, Dave, this is my Judy, and now, she's here."

"Wait, Where was this woman in the Pocono's or Philadelphia?
No sightings there."

"What are you thinking, Dave."

"I'm thinking that this whole thing is being staged. There is no way that Geremy could be on the Eastern Shores of Maryland already, traveling along the river. By tomorrow night, yes. So your person Judy is staging ahead of his arrival, and if she was not at the last two locations, how does she know where he is? So if he is working within a network, he must have to notify someone where he's going to be. Think about it. It makes sense. Imagine all the serial killers showing up at the same place at the same time."

Your making sense Dave, "the network probably has housing for these killers in remote areas throughout the country. That's how they can travel from state to state unseen."

"Who provided you the tip on Judy? I do not know it's an anonymous tip line."

"Really! Valentin, that's what we tell the public. Every call that comes in is recorded and traced back. So, where was this call from."

"It was a burner phone."

" So we do not know if we just got played."

"What do you mean?"

"What if Judy made the call. It would have been the perfect time to pull us away from the river and not observe Geremy's crossing into Maryland."

Valentins' phone rings, and it's another tip from the Judy tip line, "The tip line is telling me that Judy is in DC."

"Well, we do know that Geremy is not there yet. I'd say we have two days, and with all these additional killers, perhaps you should call in your team."

Valentin called Sullivan and delivered the new information. Sullivan notified his scattered team, and everyone was en route to Valentin's location, Aberdeen, MD. Sullivan did not want to storm into DC with an armed squad without proper notification and permission. The DC area is a beehive of law enforcement agencies. The wrong message would place hundreds of armed individuals on alert. The information had too many holes to alert DC, so it was decided for now to keep only his present team, and the Marshalls involved.

No one knew that this whole movement was a well-choreographed and directed play by the Dommes, with the perfect cast members. She provided the forged document to Geremy, sending him spiraling back to reality. She tipped the Judy line to Valentin, directly leading her to Geremy's location. What she did not foresee but worked perfectly into the plan was the addition of Dave. She would soon have everyone at the right place, this entire cell needed to be disbanded. It's been in play too long, partly because of her pride. Geremy was her best. She had fully reconditioned him, and he still held on to enough of himself for her to be attracted, intimately and emotionally.

Geremy came onshore at Slaughter Beach, DE, and fled to one of the safehouses along Bay View road and rested. In the morning, he called the number posted on the bulletin board in the hall that read 'for a Ride Dial 302-545-5377'.

This number was to an UBER, driven by another Dommes tortured fledglings. He picked up Geremy within the hour and took him to Cambridge, a small town on Maryland's eastern shores. The drop-off point was a few blocks from the waterfront safehouse. The exact location of the safe house was not known to the UBER driver. Geremy rested there until nightfall.

He commandeered a small boat docked at the pier and headed west on the Choptank River, into the Chesapeake River, then North-West to Annapolis, the location of another waterfront safehouse. He arrived three days earlier than he expected, and the travel time to DC was short. So he rested and had thoughts of how he would greet his son and Peter's first words to him.

Judy also thought why she wasn't notified about PA? Why did he leave PA early?; Why bypass Delaware? and of all the places, why come to DC? Left to her own thoughts, as a monitor, she's under one impression that he will turn himself into the DC FBI office, and it's her task to stop him.

Sullivan and agents arrived in Aberdeen the day after Geremy docked in Annapolis. Sullivan needed answers, "I know the tip on Judy brought us to DC, but can someone tell me why Geremy missed out on killing in two states to get here, and why has he not killed again? Anybody ...?

How about you, Dave? Does Geremy have family here? Is this another one of his I feel glorious moments? Somebody feed me something. If he's attempting to kill Madam President, we must alert everyone, NOW!"

Rashel looked at Dave, and he shook his head for her to be silent. Peter was due to arrive tomorrow. The silence, the lies, the imminent arrival of the boy were too much for Rashel to contain. She could not remain silent. "He thinks his son is arriving tomorrow."

Sullivan, with surprise, "Who thinks his son will arrive tomorrow? Geremy has a son?"

"No, but he thinks he has a son. Dave. It's time, tell them."

"Yes, Dave, what have you been hiding from us?"

"The part of the story that is missing from the media reports and the official records is that Angelica, the woman killed and raped in that train accident, transferred a fertile fetus to a surrogate mother that same day. Geremy was insistent that the child was his. A paternity test proved that it was not. Yet, he still believed the child to be his and swore that he and the child would be united one day. I received a call just after you made your accusation that Geremy is the serial killer, that the boy would be traveling to DC for a school trip to the Capitol. I truly hoped that we would have stopped Geremy in Delaware or Maryland, which we did not. So, I guess you're wondering why I did not tell you sooner. The child does not know how his true mother passed on; the story told him was that she died giving birth. If I had informed you of this, you would have surrounded his home and used him as a ploy to bring out Geremy. I was not going to let that happen. Several members of the US Marshalls and I have monitored this child's movement from birth, keeping in the shadows."

Dave was unaware of the media frenzy back home, which opened Peter's world to the whole story.

Sullivan was taken back by Dave's human aspect in telling the story, and all animosity between them washed away. "What do we do now, Dave? How do you want to handle this?"

"Here is what I know: The plane will land at DCA tomorrow night Southwest Flt 2432 at 5 PM. The 20 students and five chaperones will shuttle and stay overnight at the Hampton Inn & Suites at Reagan National Airport. The next morning at 9:01 AM, they will take the metro Yellow-line arriving at 9:11 AM to L'ENFANT PLAZA Metro Station. They will transfer onto the Blue-line departing at 9:22 AM, arriving at 9:26 AM to the Capitol South Metro Station, then walk to the Capitol Visitor Center for a 10 AM tour. The Capitol tour is 90 min. The itinerary is fluid from that point, several possible stops along the National Mall, Smithsonian Museums, The National Archives, The White House, and lunch. They will depart on the Blue-line at 4:16 PM from the South Capitol Metro Station, arriving back at DCA at 4:44 PM. Dinner at the Airport and depart 7:00 PM on Southwest Flt 3432."

Sullivan was pondering how to handle this. To bring armed agents into the District without prior authorization is in direct violation of Capitol policy. Still, he also knew if he reported it - it would be taken from his hands and turned into a major Capture-the-Flag scenario, possibly bringing more risk to the students and their chaperones.

"OK, everyone, listen up. We have enough people in our joint team to survey and capture Geremy, but we must execute flawlessly and stealthily. Bruce, I am assigning you to the airport, but you can not raise your FBI credentials. With that said, secure your weapon in your vehicle. Dave will provide us with a picture of the boy. I do not expect Geremy to attempt anything at the DC airport, so your role is to identify the kid and confirm that he left the airport and onto the shuttle. I doubt the Hampton Inn shuttle is equipped to take that many people at one time. Keep him under surveillance until you know he is on the shuttle and it left the curbside, then join Carmen at the hotel. Carmen, find out what floor our kid is on. Once again, no flashing of FBI credentials. You and Bruce figure out a schedule to watch the entrances and exits through the night."

Dave cuts in, "Rashel and I will take over in the morning."

Sullivan, in a softer voice this time, "Dave, he knows you. Valentin and Rashel will pick it up in the morning and stay with them on the metro. The metro stations have gun detection devices, so leave your weapons with Bruce and Carmen; you will get them back after arriving in DC. My point of concern is the events after the Capitol Tour. That is when I think he'll make his play."

Geremy started his morning with a good breakfast and a smile for what the day will bring. Dave's exact itinerary to the team was on the back of the photograph provided to Geremy from Helga. He planned to enter the city 10 mins before the ending time of the tour. Geremy had written a couple of notes to pass to Peter, explaining their relationship. He kept a slight hope that Peter would break free from the others and run away with him. Geremy called for an UBER, using the posting on the board. He directed the UBER to drop him off at 4th & C ST SW one block from the National Smithsonian Air and Space

Museum. That was the closest to the US Capital that he wanted to be dropped off. He then walked to get to a better position to view the visitor center of the US Capitol.

11:30 AM, The children came out of the tour, talking about the many statues and paintings they saw inside. They were excited to see more of DC. Their teacher was quite familiar with the DC area, having lived there for five years before moving to Sacramento. Before progressing, she had the children sit down on the US Capitol Building steps for a group picture and discuss where to go next. She was an excellent teacher and wanted her children to experience The District rather than being pulled from one place to the next. She explained the different things they had time to see, The White House. The monuments (Lincoln Memorial, Washington Memorial, and War Memorials). The museums (the Air and Space Museum, the Museum of American History, the National Museum of American Indians, the National Museum of African Americans) and The National Archives. She informed them that she would take a vote by show of hands.

"Raise your hands for your favorite as I say the name."

No surprises. They all wanted to see where the President lives; the White House, the Lincoln and Washington Memorial, and limited the Museums down to 3. Then she told them about riding a double-decker bus with the top was open to the sky to view all of the buildings as they drove by. She was referring to the Hop-On-Off bus system of touring The District. This system allows you to exit the bus at any stop and get back on any bus in the same loop at any time, a great way to view The District at your own pace seeing what you want to see. So, off they went getting onto the RED LOOP line, first stop the White House. Valentin and Rashel followed the class, riding the bus while posing as tourists.

Geremy was also aware of this bus system. He utilized the time he had gained by arriving early to acquaint himself with the many ways to maneuver in The District. There were pamphlets on sightseeing and transportation information located at the safehouse. He could follow the bus from his location, watching the class enter and exit. The travel guide on the Hop-On-Off system had a detailed map of all the loops. The RED LOOP bus map showed the White House, Lincoln Memorial, Washington Memorial, and then the National Mall Museum area. He felt that his best chance would be at the Washington Memorial, he proceeded to that RED LOOP bus stop location.

Sullivan and Dave followed the bus in their vehicle, surveying the crowds while at each stop, looking for any signs of Geremy. Onboard the bus, Valentin monitored the riders, looking for Judy. After a few hours of sleep, Carmine and Bruce rejoined the team. They were positioned ahead of the bus surveying the crowds for Geremy.

At each stop, once the class debarked from the bus, Carmine and Bruce would travel to the bus's next location, survey the crowd and wait until the bus containing the children arrived, then move to the next area. When the bus arrived at the Washington Memorial, Geremy was waiting, hiding in the shadows of the trees. Judy was a couple of feet away from Geremy, posing as another tourist. When it was time to exit the bus, Rashell went ahead of the class, and lastly, Valentin. As the bus pulled away, Judy noticed that Geremy was getting anxious, as if he were waiting for someone. She questioned herself, why would he get anxious watching children? That's when she saw Valentin and remembered her from the Florida chase.

She surmised that he would turn himself over to her, she was in a perfect location to terminate him and getaway, but she wanted to ensure his intentions. As the class lined up to wait for the next bus, Geremy started moving in that direction. He had papers in his hands. Dave noticed Geremy crossing the Raoul Wallenberg PL SW roadway from the tree-lined area. He stepped out of the car and started running towards him. Judy was behind Geremy, pulling out her gun, and as Dave began to scream out, "Geremy down," Valentin noticed Judy took one step forward, yelling, "FBI - Shooter everyone down." Rashel and Valentin were still unarmed. They ran over to shield Peter. Judy moved quickly to Geremy and fired two shots killing Geremy instantly. As she tried to flee, another shot rang out from a distance, sending some of the crowd back to the ground and others running off in all directions, ending Judy's life. Sullivan's theory of a terminator for the terminator came true, as this unseen assailant mingled amongst the many tourists and locals running and screaming to find some unknown point for safety. The second terminator ran to his vehicle parked along 14th Street. He fled the scene, turning onto Constitution Ave NW when his car doors locked and the interior burst into flames at the 16th street entrance to the White House, ending his life. It was determined later to have resulted from a small incinerating device planted under the driver's seat.

Within seconds the entire area was closed down and surrounded by DC metro, FBI, Secret Service, US Marshalls, State Parks, Capitol Police, and a few other 3 and 4 letter agents. The National Guard was alerted and moving into position. The President and first family were escorted into their strongholds. Blackhawk helicopters were arriving with fighter birds standing at the ready.

Sullivan and Dave continued running to Geremy. Carmen and Bruce returned to the scene and observed from a distance. Dave looked back to see if Peter was safe. Rashel was over him, shielding his body with hers. The children were on the ground with tears of fear rolling down their cheeks, some of them screaming, they wanted to go home while others yelled out, "is it was over," all clinging to each other as though the world was ending. Their teacher was furious, looking at the agents surrounding Peter, "What the hell is going on here? She was so consumed with the protection of her class, unable to shed any tears or show fear. "Let go of this child," pulling Peter towards her. Valentin showed her badge and explained that they received a tip of a possible kidnapping attempt on Peter. Then the borage of ringing phones filled the air, the Sacramento parents calling out to each child. The responses were deafening, "mommy, I want to go home," "Daddy, come get me," "I saw a man get shot," "I saw a lady get shot," I saw a lady shoot a man." All of the calls resulted in the children saying," Teacher, "my mom, my dad, my sister, my brother, my aunt ... want to talk to you?"

"Please, children, pass your phone to one of the chaperones. We will be on the plane tonight heading home. Everyone is safe." Agent Sullivan explained why these two ladies have been alongside the group since they left the hotel this morning.

"Why was I not informed of a possible threat to my children?"

"We were not fully certain as to the possibility of any accomplices."

"I am the teacher and the person in charge of the safety of this group. It appears that you have deliberately endangered the safety of my class to flush this man out. I will be filing a formal complaint when I get them safely home. Tell me, was Peter the only child called out in this kidnapping attempt? Does this have anything to do with the story of an escaped prisoner and the child's family?"

Dave introduced himself as a US Marshall and that this was the man that escaped from jail.

With tears flowing and trembling from the trauma, Peter overheard the conversation and asked Dave, "Is it over now? Was he the man that killed my mother?"

Dave dropped to one knee, "Hello Peter, my name is Dave. I am a friend of your family."

"Did Someone tell you about your mother's accident?"

"My Dad told me. Was that him, her friend?"

"Yes, Peter, It's all over now."

Meanwhile, the barrage of local, capital, federal and military enforcement groups were moving towards them, handcuffing Dave, Sullivan, and their team.

As the onslaught of enforcement personnel was starting to gain order amongst the chaos, one of the FBI investigative Directors noticed Sullivan and walked over to him, "Please do not tell me that this mess is part of your Dignity Reaper investigation. I am going to have your head for this. Do you have no idea how much paperwork and debriefing I will have to go through? The President was scuttled to the ready for going into lockdown. What were you thinking, not notifying this office of your presence in DC?"

The Director addressed the teacher, "Ma'am, we are sorry that this incident happened in front of your class. Would you like for us to set up counseling for the children before boarding your flight this evening?"

"I do not believe that will be necessary. We will take care of that when we get back. I do, however, not feel comfortable placing the children on buses and trains to get back to the airport."

"We have a bus coming to accommodate your group for the remainder of your trip."

All was not over yet. Helga had one more hand to play, she instructed an outside contractor to terminate the cell, and after that, she wanted to remove the one person that kept Geremy from being fully committed to her. She wanted the boy killed. The hired contractor had Peter in his sights, waiting for a clear shot.

At that moment, an alert came across the field radios, "We have a heat signature on top of the Sidney Yates Federal Building that should not be there. Federal authorities have been dispatched with orders to catch alive if possible. Dave, hearing them talk, shouted, shooter, protect Peter. Shots were heard in the distance, followed by another radio alert, "Shooter Neutralized, repeat Shooter Neutralized."

The students and chaperones were loaded onto the bus, and the police escorted them through the streets of DC to all the places they wanted to see, and they were treated to pizza and ice cream. Then, they were driven directly to the aircraft and entered via the outside stair exit before any other passengers.

The FBI team and Marshalls were detained for several hours, well into the evening being debriefed. Carmen and Bruce were released first under the guise of just following orders. Rashel and Valentin were suspended for a month. Rashell left the US Marshalls and joined the FBI, where, together with Valentin were assigned the task to flush out these domestic terrorist networks. Sullivan was praised in the media for ending the killings of the Dignity Reaper. The FBI sent him back to his foreign assignment

Days after all of the accusations of misuse of power and not following proper governmental protocols were over. Dave was forced out of the US Marshalls. He accepted the panel's determination with open arms, for, with the death of his friend and the memory of his body lying before him, he found his inner peace. Dave's drive was to capture Geremy, not to kill him. He wanted to continue the intervention that they (he and Carl) started so many years prior. His thought was that one day, while incarcerated and receiving psychiatric help, Geremy would wake up out of this dark dream that was possessing him and acknowledge what he had done. That vision was all gone now, and Dave had no further desire to be a part of a law enforcement unit. He now understood Jasmine's reasoning for not going back, and just like their love story started, she welcomed him back to her arms to stay.

Dave had collected the papers that Geremy had in his hands the day Judy shot him. One of these was the forgery of the paternity judgment, which Dave gave to Rashell for her investigations. The others were letters to Peter. The Peter letters were not encouraging Peter to run away with him. Instead, they were letters of a father talking to his son. They were his confessions; Why he could not be that Dad of your dreams, What happened that day on the train, What it meant to Geremy to be his father, How happy he was to know that Peter was safe and had good people around him, that loved him, and finally, Why your father must now go away and not bring you with him?

Geremy's delusions of having a son were indeed his final salvation, bringing the strength to break his mental bondage and finally reach back up to the tight-rope.

~~~ One Too Many Drinks ~~~
~~~